Arthur Gray Butler

Charles I.

A tragedy in five acts

Arthur Gray Butler

Charles I.
A tragedy in five acts

ISBN/EAN: 9783337105907

Printed in Europe, USA, Canada, Australia, Japan

Cover: Foto ©Andreas Hilbeck / pixelio.de

More available books at **www.hansebooks.com**

CHARLES I.

A TRAGEDY in FIVE ACTS

BY

ARTHUR GRAY BUTLER, M.A.

FELLOW OF ORIEL COLLEGE, OXFORD

LONDON

LONGMANS, GREEN, AND CO.

1874

'He nothing common did or mean
Upon that memorable scene,
    But with his keener eye
    The axe's edge did try;
Nor called the gods, with vulgar spite,
To vindicate his helpless right;
    But bowed his comely head
    Down, as upon a bed.'

A. MARVELL.

PREFACE.

THE SCENE of this play is laid at first at Hampton Court, where Charles, with the consent of the generals of the victorious army, was living in the month of August, 1647. All seemed at last to shine upon him. His old courtiers, Richmond, Hertford, Southampton, Ormond, Berkeley, Ashburnham, and others, had been permitted to rejoin him ; and there, amid the pomp and splendour of a court, he soon regained the confidence which had been only for a moment shaken by defeat. Yet his difficulties, could he have really apprehended them, were never greater. It is true that the dissensions of the Army and Parliament had reached their height. It is true that each of them was bidding separately for his acceptance of their terms : the Parliament to secure the triumph of the Presbyterian cause ; the Army, filled with zealots of every kind, both in politics and religion, to maintain them-selves in arms, to secure full liberty of worship, and to prevent the establishment of a system which they hated only less bitterly than Episcopacy. But had Charles possessed any insight, he would have been alarmed

rather than flattered at this competition for his favour.
The rivalry of two such antagonists ensured him a bitter
enemy in the one whom he did not choose for his ally.
If, siding with the Army, he returned to power by their
aid, and on their terms, he would have alienated all that
was moderate and order-loving in the kingdom. Most
of all he would have alienated his own devoted followers,
who would have considered such an alliance as Apostasy,
and the obligations thus incurred to Cromwell as more
humiliating than even exile or imprisonment. But if, on
the other hand, he had heartily and unreservedly ac-
cepted the proposals made to him by the Parliament,
how would he have been enabled to overcome the oppo-
sition of the Army, and its ambitious leaders? He was
at that time a prisoner in their hands, violently seized,
though honourably detained by them. How could he
expect to go forth from that captivity without the full
consent of the unscrupulous men who had brought him
there ; who, even amid the state with which they had
surrounded him, never allowed him to forget for long
that they were his masters, not he theirs?

This dangerous position of the King has not been
sufficiently attended to. It has been assumed that he
had only to embrace the proposals made to him by one
or other of the two great victorious parties in the State ;
and that then all his difficulties would have vanished.
On the contrary, it seems to me, they would have been
increased tenfold. The great majority of Charles's opponents belonged to the Presbyterian party, who wished to

enforce their religious system upon all. The Army re-
presented a small minority in the nation, only rendered
formidable by its valour, its fanaticism, the proud con-
sciousness of its services, and, above all, by the genius of
Cromwell. What hope, then, of peace and settlement in
the presence of parties so embittered, so intolerant, so
irreconcilable? The Sects hated the Presbyterians :
the Presbyterians the Sects : both equally hated, and
were hated by, the Episcopalians. It was one of those
critical periods of history, when great principles come
into the sharpest conflict, and when, compromise and
toleration not being understood, bitter and endless war-
fare is inevitable. It was Charles's misfortune to have
been born at such a time. It was his fault that by his
weakness, his insincerity, his inability to understand the
times, and his incapacity either to guide or to control
them, be aggravated to the uttermost difficulties which
would have severely tasked the powers of any king, however wise and patriotic.

But I am not writing a life of Charles, much less an
essay on the Rebellion. Merely I wish it to be understood how perplexing even to a great statesman was
the position in which the King found himself after the
defeat of Naseby ; and how perplexing no less was that
of the other great parties in the State. Where compromise is not admitted into the councils of a nation,
peace and harmony are impossible. We have to thank
the great Rebellion, among other things, for one priceless

lesson in politics which will never be forgotten—of the
necessity and wisdom of compromise.

But still admitting the great perplexity of Charles's cir-
cumstances, we must insist strongly on the extreme folly
and blindness of his conduct. He was by nature very
undecided, and, like all undecided men, greatly under
the influence of advisers and events. He was also of a
buoyant and sanguine disposition, ever ready to expect
the best for himself; while his high notions of prerogative, and belief in his Divine Right, made him at once
averse to all concession, and unwilling to believe that a
power resting on supernatural foundations could ever fall.

And so he allowed his Court to become a centre for
every kind of negotiation and intrigue. Lauderdale
and Lanark besought him to join the Presbyterians, and
even promised the support of a strong Scottish force.
Cromwell and Ireton urged him to join them and the
Army openly; declaring that they would in that case
force their conditions upon the Parliament, conditions
more favourable to the King than any others hitherto
proposed to him. Charles listened to both parties, and
wavered between them. He listened also to his own
courtiers and flatterers, who were reckless and arrogant
as ever; and secretly fomented insurrections among the
northern Cavaliers, ordering them to be ready to fly to
arms at the fitting moment, and take advantage of the
dissensions now raging amid their enemies.

In the general disturbance then impending Charles
thought that something must turn up favourable to

himself and to his cause. He never dreamt of any
danger that could befall his own sacred person.

How blind, how insensate such conduct was, we now
see most clearly. In all the intrigues, in all the plottings
and schemings, in all the calculations of the King, one
most important consideration was forgotten. He was in
the power of the Army. He was in the power of men,
who had bought success dearly with their blood, and
were little disposed to see its fruits stolen from them by
the intrigues of the enemy whom they had conquered.
Already they had been taught to regard him as a wicked
and idolatrous king, who was striving to corrupt their
simple faith, and lead them back again to the false
worship which their forefathers had abjured. Already,
too, they were murmuring at him as the cause of all the
miseries which had befallen the unhappy nation. But
now, when there seemed a danger of all these miseries
being renewed, they believed themselves to have reached
one of those periods recorded in Sacred History, when
punishment has to be inflicted on selfish and wilful kings,
whom for their sins God has visited with blindness; and
there began to arise among them a stern cry for vengeance, with muttered denunciations against the generals
who, forgetting their higher calling, were stooping to the
fear of man, and making themselves the instruments of a
carnal and crooked policy. The King did not, or would
not, hear these mutterings, indications of the coming
storm. Cromwell and Ireton heard them, and were once
more most urgent with him, and apparently in good faith,

to give them his entire confidence, and to range himself wholly on their side. He continued to waver, swayed to and fro by contending motives. His mind, naturally more speculative than practical, more reflective than observing, could neither read the persons nor the times amid which he was cast. Events, ludicrously unimportant, seemed to him of the greatest significance. Powers, obviously inadequate to attain his end, appeared to his imagination stronger than all his enemies put together. And his pride, supported by nobler feelings of obligation to his Church and Crown, could not bear to confess itself beaten. And lastly, he recoiled with all the repugnance of a king, a Churchman, and a fastidious gentleman, from the levelling principles, the irregular and daring worship, and the narrow prejudices of the Puritan and Independent schools.

It was in some humour of this kind, very possibly a passing humour, that he wrote the famous letter, very probably inspired by some incident of the moment, which I have embodied in the Play. By some the letter is attributed to the Queen, not to Charles. By others it is considered to be an entire fiction, invented by Charles's enemies. But there seems reason to believe in its existence, and that it was written by Charles in confidential communication with his fond but ill-advising Queen. Certainly it explains the sudden and decisive change in Cromwell's conduct. 'The two generals,' says Guizot, 'looked at each other after reading the King's letter, and, all their suspicions thus confirmed, returned to

Windsor, henceforward as free from uncertainty respecting their designs upon the King, as respecting his towards them.'

Immediately their treatment of the royal prisoner altered. His courtiers were ordered to leave him; his guards were doubled; his liberty was abridged: until at last, a prey to the darkest fears and anxieties, the un-happy Charles fled away to the Isle of Wight, and entrusted himself to Colonel Hammond, governor of the island, the nephew of his most devoted chaplain.

Then began his second captivity, and the different steps leading to his trial and death followed in quick succession.

One more intrigue with the Scotch, whose forces, commanded by the Duke of Hamilton, and aided by Langdale and his Cavaliers, were promptly beaten and dispersed by Cromwell; one more prolonged negotiation at Newport, rendered fruitless by the determination of the King not to give up the Church of England; and then once more Charles was carried off by the agents of the army, first to Hurst Castle and then to Windsor, whence he was soon after removed to London to undergo his trial, and meet his death. From this time all that was noble in the King's character began to show itself without alloy. Never was there a man more fitted to undergo suffering with patience, or to meet accusations in a dignified and touching manner. His pride was great. It had led him to the most extravagant notions of his prerogative. It had thus, by necessitating an armed resistance, been the cause of countless miseries to the nation. Even after his defeat, by the stubbornness with which he clung to every hope of regaining his lost power, it had irritated his enemies to the uttermost. But when they, exasperated at the last beyond measure, proceeded to take vengeance on him for his obstinacy, then the pride, which had been his worst enemy, became his best friend, and, elevated by religion, enabled aim to bear all with matchless fortitude and constancy.

As to the great question of his execution, men's minds will ever be divided. It is impossible to deny that he was a bad king, and that his high notions of prerogative were incompatible with the freedom of his people. It is impossible, also, to overlook the difficulty of knowing what to do with him. And yet, if Cromwell had not so weakened the authority of Parliament as to make it contemptible, and raised the Army into an independent position, it is possible that the united majesty of these two powers might have awed even Charles into submission. As it was, their dissensions fatally encouraged his intrigues.

As to the tribunal which tried the King, no unprejudiced person can maintain its legality. It was a tribunal of violence. Its sentence was dictated by the sword. It was shocking to the great law-loving majority of the nation. And it was the horror thus excited, quite as much as men's impatience of a government of force like Cromwell's, which paved the way for the Restoration, and with it for a flood of reactionary servility both in

Church and State. Excesses provoke excesses; and freedom suffers where its enemies find an assistant in the remorseful silence of its friends.

But if we thus judge of the King's death, what excuse is to be made for Cromwell, on whom lies the real responsibility of the measure? Is not Cromwell the Protector, with his calm good sense and magnificent ruling power, the best evidence against Cromwell the Regicide? He surely was not deceived by the arguments of his fanatical followers. He must have seen that the death of Charles would ultimately increase rather than remove his difficulties; and that needless bloodshed would only prejudice his cause.

Our answer to this question must depend much on our estimate of Cromwell—a character of infinite complexity, combining the strength, and width, and passion of a great Englishman with the narrow but intense faith of a fervent Puritan; full of aspirations towards the unseen world, yet with the clearest insight into the laws of action and success in this. In such a character it is inevitable that contradictions should occur, especially in troublous times of change. Sometimes magnanimous, sometimes seemingly revengeful; sometimes running over with high animal spirits, at other times oppressed with melancholy; with a strong desire for sympathy and to be loved, and yet trampling upon men's interests and prejudices, fearlessly, at every turn; self-willed and obstinate, but looking for heavenly guidance even in the details of policy; eager, as a patriot, for the honour of England, but seeking, as a Puritan, God's honour above all : such is the picture of this extraordinary man given us from various sources, a hopeless task to represent (even had I the power) in a work primarily devoted to his rival.

And yet I think that no one can have read Cromwell's letters and speeches, lighted up by the flashes of Carlyle's genius, without the feeling, growing almost to conviction on the whole, that the man was sincere : that he had before him the noblest of all aims, the establishment of freedom and religion on a firm basis : and though many of his acts need apology, yet they were prompted by no base or selfish motive, but from the desire that a great cause should not suffer in his hands. The key to explain his actions is the belief, shared in common with his whole party, that they were under the special guidance of Providence ; employed as instruments to work out a pre-ordained plan, whose details were revealed to them by the Spirit, when the appointed time was come. Woe to the man who then allowed his weak human feelings to stand in the way of the great purpose of the Lord! It was the sin of Saul sparing Agag, and the chief of the things which ought to have been destroyed, out of mere pity, or vanity, or miserable motives of expediency.

Such is fanaticism, a creed which supposes fallible man to have in him an infallible guide : a frightfully dangerous creed, when, passing from speculation into practice, it has to deal with party-interests, or questions involving private gain. In such cases the world's cynical test of the fanatic's honesty, ' What had he to get by it?' is often only too applicable. No man is a safe decider in his own case. Reason then becomes the advocate, instead of the impartial judge.

And yet the test is, like all rough methods of gauging human action, far from being perfect. Above all, it fails in the case of Cromwell, by putting out of sight the noble and unselfish cause for which he had been fighting, as well as the boiling passionate character, often, we are told, venting itself in sobs and tears, of the man himself. It is cold, selfish, calculating characters to which the test of ' What had he to get by it?' may safely be applied.

In the case of Cromwell and the Independents a truer test would be, Was such a course in accordance with their traditions, with the tenets of their religious school, with the principles which governed their daily lives? Were their virtues, as well as their crimes, fruits of the same original stock of superstition? If so, however much we may condemn their principles, we may not question their general honesty. And judged by this test, and this alone, Cromwell's reputation comes off unscathed. Our estimate of his intellectual greatness may be lowered: but the old charge of hypocrisy and self-seeking ambition tumbles to the ground. And so, when he says, as he did say in Parliament, ' that Providence and necessity had led them to the trial of the King,' he did not distinguish, as we do now, between these two opposites. To the Predestinarian, what is

divinely ordered is necessary: and inversely, what is
necessary is divinely ordered. Man is not left to his
own guidance. He has an infallible inner light to guide
him; and where it goes before, and points the way, he
must follow. 'Ought' and 'must' to him are not two,
but one.

And yet my belief is that Cromwell long wavered as
to this decisive step. He did not see his way. That
intensity of combined conviction and feeling, which was
to him the guidance of the Spirit, had not yet come.
'If anyone,' he said in the speech before quoted, 'had
moved this trial upon design, I should think him the
greatest traitor in the world; but since Providence and
necessity have cast us on it, I pray God to bless our
counsels, though I am not prepared on the sudden to
give my advice.' Humanity, moderation, pity for a
fallen adversary, foresight of consequences, still struggled
in his mind against the sombre dictates of fanaticism.
But at length, infected by the prevailing madness of his
followers, and zealous as an ancient prophet for the
triumph of his cause, he threw himself into the new
movement with his accustomed ardour. It was the
finger of God which had led them from their low estate
to the giddy height on which they then stood. It was
the voice of God which then called them to complete
their victory.

Now if this be the right view to take of Cromwell's
conduct upon this occasion, it will be seen at once how
much there is in common, strange to say, between him

and Charles. Extremes meet. Each believed his cause, his right, his mission to be divine; and each was thus led to do things which otherwise his sober reason would have disapproved. And the moral of it is plain, that whoever thinks himself or his cause so necessary to the world, that common principles of right and prudence may be overlooked, is treading in a dangerous path, and sooner or later he is sure to fall into the dark abysses of fanaticism. On the necessity of thus weighing the two great adversaries in one impartial scale we cannot insist too strongly. It will not do to denounce the egotism and insincerity of Charles, unless we are prepared also to condemn the unscrupulousness and violence of Cromwell. Both were zealots and fanatics, the one in the cause of liberty, the other of authority. Neither of them would submit their claims to the verdict of the majority of the country, the only tribunal which can adjust the balance between such opponents. And the consequences that thus befell the great body of the nation were most disastrous. A self-willed General, who believes himself or his party to be infallible, may be as dangerous to freedom as the self-willed Monarch who believes his right to be divine.

In taking this view, and trying to hold the scales fairly between the contending parties, I have had to sacrifice somewhat of dramatic unity and intensity. The events are too near, the characters too dear to us, to admit of their being shifted and moved about at will, as pawns upon the dramatic chessboard. We may not construct

a

scenes and characters out of our own imagination, and
then, as has been said, 'do some historical events or
personages the compliment of borrowing their names.'
Even where invention is permitted, it must be within
narrow bounds, and jealously guarded from transgression.

But one chief object of the Play will be attained if it
lead partisans of either side to appreciate the nobleness
of their opponents, of their main principles at all events,
if not of their actions ; if it lead them to weigh the repre-
sentatives of these principles in that generous balance
applicable to a period of revolution; if it induce the
belief that erring and imperfect lives are most fairly judged
by the general motives by whose light they steered,
rather than by the occasional tackings and variations of
their course.

And at the same time, while making allowance for
men too staggered by the shocks of change and the
rush of new ideas to preserve always an even course, let
us not forget those great men, their contemporaries,
whose career was less chequered, less questionable, who
never stooped to violence to pick up an apparent advantage, nor abandoned principles because doubtful of their
triumph.

These men, the Constitutionalists, the Hampdens, the
Falklands, the moderate party of all ages, the Girondins
of a later revolution, are not indeed fitted to shine in
the eyes of men who wait on Fortune and reserve their
admiration for success. Oftener than not they perish in
exile, or by the guillotine, or the hand of the assassin ;

or they are 'laughed down and disappear' before zealots less scrupulous and more uncompromising.

And yet they are the real heroes of the time they live in. It is to them that statues should be raised by a free people. It is to their purer virtues we should turn with reverence, recoiling from the picturesque attractions of a strong Government, whether of Absolute Monarchy or Military Despotism. And when the deluge subsides, it is on their principles that order is re-established; and their doctrines, little heeded when uttered, become the watchwords of reviving Constitutional Liberty.

DRAMATIS PERSONÆ.

King Charles the First.

Earl of Ormond.

Lord Ashburnham, and Herbert : *Attendants of the King.*

Lord Digby : *Attendant on the Queen.*

Juxon, *Bishop of London.*

Oliver Cromwell.

John Cromwell.

John Milton.

Earl of Denbigh.

General Ireton.

Lord Fairfax.

Ludlow,
Hutchinson,
Lambert,
Wychcott, } *Colonels in the Parliamentary Army.*
Downs,
Axtell,
Huncks,

Hugh Peters, *Chaplain to the Army.*

Ephraim Saint-Good : *Puritan Soldier.*

Richard, *a Countryman.*

A Falconer : A Butler.

Two Tavern Keepers.

Henrietta Maria, *Queen of Charles I.*

Lady in waiting to the Queen.

Princess Elizabeth, and Duke of Gloucester.

Lady Fairfax.

Mrs. Cromwell, and Mrs. Claypole, *Cromwell's Daughter.*

Scene is laid first at Hampton Court, and then in London.

CHARLES THE FIRST.

A DRAMA IN FIVE ACTS.

---◦◦◦---

ACT I.

SCENE I.—IN FRONT OF HAMPTON COURT.

A FALCONER: *a* BUTLER: SERVANTS *of the* KING :
Roundhead soldiers, country people.

Return of hunting party.

Falconer. Well, Mr. Roundhead, I told you the King
should enjoy his own again. I say, I told you so, by the
token that you had me fined for swearing it: and now
see if it be not come true. We never had such a day's
sport since I can remember, and that's fifty good years
come Lady day. Master Butler, a cup of good ale after
a day's hard work——

Butler. Will keep a falconer from the ague. By St.
George, and you shall have one of the best, Will ; though
there were an Act of Parliament against it. Out of the
way, good people ! out of the way ! Never make a fat
man go round, when he can go straight. Thank you,
gentlemen, thank you.   [*Exit.*

Falc. Three noble herons, and a heronshaw ! Jack

B

Roundhead, there's a day's sport for you. Look here now, here's a gallant crest : 'tis the good bird's lovelock : for Nature is and ever has been a cavalier, and (*humming*) 'is all for cavaliers, true and hearty cavaliers.' Would you crop Nature too, and have her turn roundhead?

Soldier. Yet did this gallant crest not save the good bird from the falcon.

Falc. Out, ruffian! will ye liken yourselves to falcons? The falcon is a gentleman, Jack : and that is what you will never be.

Sold. There are better things than gentlemen in the world.

Falc. Where do they grow? In the most righteous and godly army? among the most pious and upright Parliament? Old England will never get fat off them. Show Will Harding one of these gentry, and he'll show you a psalm-singing canting hypocrite. Pah! They wear Christ's livery, but they're the Devil's serving-men.

Sold. Keep a civil tongue, or——

Falc. It will be the worse for me. I know it ; and so

I'll be civil as the devil
When he's talking to his own.   [*Aside.*

So, truss thyself, my pretty bird (*to his falcon*). The King has praised thee for thy work this day. Oh, 'tis a noble sport.

Sold. 'Tis a profane pastime.

Falc. As bad as a Maypole on a village green or a swarm of bees on Sunday! Come, come, friend! Serve God and be cheerful! Why Noll himself loves a good hawk, and a good hound : so we have authority for our sin.

Sold. Would that were the only vanity that the General is snared by ; but his heart wanders from the truth like a brook by the wayside.

Falc. Let's shake hands over that text ! Two roads and one end ! If you hate him, sure I am that I do.

Sold. Verily——

Falc. Verily here comes the Butler.

Butl. With a powerful drink, dear Will, that will make the eyes stare in your head like beacons for a royal victory. (*Gives it him.*) That's the way : that's the way. Let the flagon's bottom see the sun ! Isn't that a good drink now? Good enough for the King, God bless him ?

Butl. By St. Nicholas ! But 'tis wine.

Falc. Hush. Hark in thy ear. These rascally knaves get none of that tap. This to that, if I may say so, this to that is nectar to ditchwater. Ha, ha ! And they never know the difference.

Falc. We'll have a toast : tell me not it's against the law ! and a song : tell me not it's profane ! I say, we'll have a toast and a song, and all of you, d'ye hear, join in. (*Sings.*)

Come a bumper to the King, let us fill, let us fill !
Let the canting rascals say what they will, what they will,
For to all but a fool it is plain, very plain,
That the King shall enjoy his own again, again, again ;
That the King shall enjoy his own again.

[*People join in.*

And here's his Majesty's health, God bless him.

2 Soldier. Do you know, friend, what a knock on the head means.

Falc. Surely. It means a big hulking fellow, with a face as sour as crab-apples, and a fist would knock down a bullock.

3 *Sold.* He shall go before the magistrate for toast-drinking.

Falc. A fig for your magistrates! The King will be here directly.

Butl. Come, Mr. Nehemiah Holdfast! leave every man to his own way! You keep the whine in your noses (*snuffling*), and we'll keep our noses in the wine (*drinking*).

Soldiers. Shall we stand this?

         [*They seize him: then trumpet sounds.*

Butl. Peace! Here comes his Majesty!

Enter KING CHARLES, *attended. The* EARL *of* ORMOND, LORD ASHBURNHAM.

Orm. See they maltreat our people.

K. Charles.   How, they dare?
Here in our palace? Now, by Holy Church,
Let go my servant—

Sold. He has broken law,
And must be punished.

K. Charles.   And I, who am the law,
Bid you release him. So!   [*They let him go.*

Ashb. When the King speaks
Treason is dumb.

People. God save your Majesty!

         [*The Butler presents a letter, which the King*
            looks at, and puts joyfully in his bosom.

K. Charles. Come nearer, friends! Methought I heard a strain
Of late too unfamiliar to my ear,

Used to the rude jars of captivity.

Oh, prythee, sound that carol once again !

Falc. Nay another verse, your Majesty. ·You would not have us like those canting Roundheads, with their damnable repetitions.

Come a blessing on the cause, let us sing, let us sing ;
As for Roundheads in the halter let them swing, let them swing ;
For to all, &c.

K. Charles. Sounds not their strain prophetic, Ashburnham ?

Ashb. It doth, my Liege. Pray Heaven it may be so.

K. Charles. As the first pipe of sun-saluting birds, ·
After the passing of the thunderstorm.

(*Advancing.*) And now, goodnight. I thank you for
    your love.   [*Crowd disperse, with shouts.*

K. Charles (*turning to his suite*). The evening air
    breathes sweetly. See, my lords,

Yon sinking sun fills all the sky with glory,

Whose majesty at noon was cloaked in clouds,

Hiding its fair perfections. So anon,

Long hid, long clouded, yet persistent still,

From veils of calumny shines Virtue forth

Conqueror at last.

Ormond.   So too a monarch comes,

By sorrow or by sickness long obscured,

To grace once more some glorious festival :

Then are his people glad at seeing him :

Then smiles he, and his smile is mirror'd round :

Bends his proud head, and every heart is stirred :

Speaks to them, falteringly protests his love,

His truth, his zeal, his fire (a knife that cut

Into his own fond bosom), making days,
Sadly spent absent from them, years : yet all,
All compensated by that single hour :
And then, amid that happy weeping throng,
So loud erewhile in murmurs, full of snarls,
None but would hold life cheap ; to lose it nothing ;
For such a prince too poor an offering.

    K. Charles.   Thanks, my good Ormond : but—I
      know thy love.
And now our game !

    Ormond.   Here, Sire, the falconer stands,
With hawk on wrist, and many a heron below.

    K. Charles. Come, let us see ! Good fellow bring
      your game.
See you this heron ? take it to Sion House :
There are my children, tied, poor sweet hearts, fast
In cruel fetters : say, I sent it to them ;
Say that I love them : and then note them well.
Look their cheeks pale and haggard (mark them well),
Channell'd with tears, like ivory tempest-worn ?
Start they at sound of kindness ? have they learnt
Suspicion's evil art, to feign, to lie,
Seeming in all ? mask that on manhood sits
Most shameful, but on childhood's simple grace
Sadder than angels fallen ? O my sweet babes—
But hush ! what say I, clouding this our joy
With words ill-omen'd ? Hence. Return with speed.

    Falc. I will be there and back before the morn. [*Exit.*

    K. Charles.   Good ! now to business ! I could
      laugh at care :
All shines so brightly. Come, good Ashburnham !

                           [*Exeunt.*

SCENE II.—ROOM IN A PALACE, IN PARIS.

QUEEN *and* LADY *in Waiting.*

Queen. Venez, ma mignonne, come and sit by me.

Lady. Are you sick, Lady? ·

Queen.   No, not sick, but sad!

O Charles, Charles, Charles, why do you leave me here?

Sing me some song!

Lady.   My harp is out of tune.

Queen. What, there too discord? discord everywhere?

Yet sing!

Lady.   Of what?

Queen.   Of love, of happy love.

Lady. Love in the spheres?

Queen.   No, in a cottage born;

Mid simple blisses hiving sweet content,

Where comes no breath of envy, no regret,

Nor murmurs, save the rivulet in the vale.

Lady. This love I know not. What I know I sing-

Song.

In the days when Earth was young,
    Love and Laughter roamed together:
Love took up his harp and sung,
    Round him all was golden weather.
But there came a sigh anon—
What will be when Life is gone?

Laughter then would try his skill,
    Sang of mirth and joy undying:
But he played his part so ill,
    He set Echo all a-sighing.
Ever came an undertone—
What will be when Life is done

Then for ever since that time,
   Love no more can live with Laughter :
For bright as is the Summer-prime,
   Winter pale will follow after,
Love henceforth must dwell with Sighs :
Joy was left in Paradise.

Queen. The song is sad, and yet the words are gay.

Lady. Lady, I cannot sing love's happiness.

Queen. How so?

Lady.   Love's ways are all a labyrinth.
Some in his mazes meet, and know it not ;
And some well-knowing meet to part in tears,
Through barriers broken-hearted. Sweet sad lot !
And some with Hero's heart, Leander's fire,
Go to their grave, nor ever find a soul
Twin with their own : but die and leave the world,
Life's sweetest word unspoken.

Queen.   Ah, poor child !
So learned in love's lore ! Who taught you ? Girl,
Have you a lover ?

Lady.   Madam !

Queen.   If you have,
Bid him not live in England ! 'Tis a land,
Whose sons are cruel, cold, and treacherous.

Lady. Lady, if some were traitors, some were true.

Queen. They were. And now what are they ?
    Cromwell's slaves !

Lady. Not all ! That are not all. My father, madam—

Queen. Died for his king, I know it. But we argue
Too much. What is't o'clock ?

Lady.   It is the hour
Lord Digby should be here.

Queen.   Our messenger !
Quick, pen and paper ! (*Writes.*)
                    Charles, Oh hadst thou followed
My counsel, England had been tame ere now.
Saw you e'er Strafford, girl ?
Lady.   No, Madam, never.
Queen. That was the man to govern Englishmen.
A will of iron ! Would you had seen him ! Strange,
He had the finest hands in all the world.[1]
But hark, who comes ! Lord Digby ? Good my lord,

Enter LORD DIGBY.

You are for England ?
Digby.   Madam, if the wind
Prosper my sail, to-morrow's setting sun
Sees me in England.
Queen.   Execrable land !
Yet oh ! were I but there ! This to the King !
To Hampton Court ! My tenderest love to him !
Say, I am weary of my banishment,
Bid him make peace !
Digby.   On all conditions ?
Queen.   No,
Upon condition that he reign a king !
Else let him reign alone ! I will stay here.
Digby. I'll tell him, Lady. Fear not, he is firm.
Queen. And firmness brings round all things to itself ;
They cannot do without him.
Digby.   Be assured,
He will be firm.

[1] See Appendix.

Queen.   Yet let him not too stiffly
Stick at a name !   The Bishops, let him yield
Their claims a little !   God will guard his own.

     Digby.   And the Militia !

     Queen.   Never !   No, my lord !
Not the Militia !   Let him cling to that
As to his life.   Who has the sword has power.
With it we can have vengeance, win back all.
Without it, Kings their subjects' scapegoats are,
Outcast for their offendings.

     Digby.   But if, Madam——

     Queen. But if ! Why will you thwart me ? You are free,
Lord Digby ! free to visit England.   You
Can see at will your loved ones.   I alone,
A Queen, wife, daughter, mother of a King,
Must live in exile : never to see more
Husband, or home, or children.   Is this well !
Each fanatic may call me Jezebel,
And lust to send me whither Strafford, Laud,
Were sent before me.   Is this well again ?
No, peace, peace, peace, but to make after war !
Now gracious words ! then bloodiest chastisement !

     Digby.   Madam, I will inform him of your wishes :
And trust you may his better angel prove,
To save him from worse fortunes.

     Queen.   Quick, away !
Each moment that delays me of my good
Is as an age of pain in a dress of fire.

                    [*Exit* LORD DIGBY.
Girl, we shall soon set foot again in England.

     Lady.   And then all will be happy.

Queen.   No, not all.

Lady.   How?

Queen.   Some must suffer.

Lady.   Will you not have mercy?

Queen.   Mercy on them, *ces misérables !* You ask me !
Mignonne, if you had Cromwell at your feet,
What would you do?

Lady.   I know not.

Queen.   I would crush him :
And with him all his baseborn followers.

Lady.   Madam, the English are a stubborn race.

Queen.   Then stubbornness must be their government.   [*Exeunt.*

SCENE III.—A ROOM AT HAMPTON COURT.

IRETON and Soldiers in background.

Iret.   To see the snare, yet listen to the lure !
Blindly to follow where the butcher leads
Right on into the shambles !   Not deceived,
Yet let deception mock us to our beards !
Is not this madness, madness fitting men
Dwellers in Bedlam, not victorious chiefs,
The boldest hands that ever drew the sword?
                                [*Enter* CROMWELL.

Crom.   Where is the guard?   Turn out !   Show me
    your pieces !
Have you your matches?   Is your powder dry?

Simeon.   Truly yes, General.

Crom.   What, old Simeon? recovered from thy
wound already !

Sim. It was but a fleshwound, General, a mere scratch.

Crom. Ha, ha! They cut steel with pen-knives when they slash my Ironsides! Pen-knives against steel. And thou, Reuben! How goes it, old comrade? Rememberest thou our last charge together?

Reu. Aye, General, it was on Naseby field.

Crom. It was, friend, it was. And how we drove them that day! how we drove them, like to chaff before the wind! It was a great mercy, a crowning mercy. That will do. Be ready, men, be ready. Ye know not when the hour will come. We have an enemy within as well as without. Be ready! '(*They retire, he turns and sees* IRETON). What, Ireton, black as thunder! What has happened?

Iret. Tell me, why deal we farther with the King?

Crom. 'Tis needful, Ireton.

Iret. Needful? for what cause?
He loves us not, but only uses us
As the rich client doth his poor attorney,
A necessary vermin to unearth,
Vermin yet baser still.

Crom. I say, 'tis needful.

Ireton. He has the Jesuit poison in his blood,
And knows their cursed canons far too well,
'Ends hallow means,' 'No faith with infidels'!
Yet oft deceived we wait upon him still,
As men bent on self-murder. What still needful?
Nay, if thou lend an ear to every need,
Thou wilt thyself become a beggar, Cromwell.

Crom.   Come hither, unbeliever; here, look forth !
                    [*Leading him to the window.*
See you yon star?
Iret.   I see no star, but clouds.
Crom.   And yet I see it, Ireton.
Iret.   How?
Crom.   'Tis there.
But you who see with eyes, and not with faith,
You cannot see it.
Iret.   This is ecstasy.
Crom.   Mock it not, Ireton ! 'Tis a higher sense
Than all your seeing blindness.   Nay, my friend,
Think not I love his many-winding ways !
But if——
Ireton.   If men of brambles gather grapes,—
We know the rest.   Look, Cromwell, first at home !
Study our needs !   The Scotsman buzzing war :
Capel and Langdale and Sir Richard Musgrave
Up in the North : the whole army mutinous ;
Leaders and all, sedition's very hive :
Bold Robert Lilburne, Rainsborough, and Harrison
Backing and leading them ; and all this done
With the good King a-gazing from his window,
Like gluttony upon a growing feast,
Smiling approval l   Does not, I say, all this
Condemn our folly's drift, and cry, Give o'er?
        Crom.   Cleverly argued. lawyer on thy brief l
Yet stay, and to the eye of thy discerning
Let me too picture these our varied times.
We seek the peace and liberties of England :
A noble aim, the heart runs fire to feel it.

But liberty's a many-meaning word,
Worth much or little as the lips that use it.
The King would have it but a playing child,
Held in the leading-strings of Mother Church.
The Parliament would have it more a man,
But conscience-fettered by the Platform's rule.
But we—we would be free in conscience also,
Knowing no fetters but our own free mind.
Authority, that is a grandam's story ;
Freedom, that is my heaven-enlightened soul :
My light, the God within me, my sole guide.
It, it or nothing : no concession there !

    Iret.   All this I grant : so far we are agreed.

    Crom.   Well, thinkest thou, Ireton, that in gracious
       mood
The Parliament will grant us liberty ?
The Formalist to Independence yield ?
The Presbyter set free the Sectary ?
Never ! we must enforce it from the King :
Then, as we won it, keep it with our swords.

    Iret.   Yes, with our swords.   I trust them, not his
      words.

    Crom.   To brittle iron ?

    Iret.   More brittle faith of kings !

    Crom.   Aye, true !   And they would train our con-
      sciences,
Who trick us at their will.   O princes, princes,
Because our bodies yield you temporal service,
Kneeling in awestruck homage 'neath your throne,
How dare you, what is throned above you fetter,
The mystery of a soul ?   My purse is Cæsar's,

My service, and my sword : let Cæsar take them,
Command my reverence, and in the murderous field
Send me to death. All shall be bearable.
But this, to admit a lie into my soul,
To adulterate my spirit's inmost being,
Feign where I feel, bend where I have not bowed
The homage of my heart—ere I do this,
And in my bosom's pure devoted temple,
Made for the Holiest, let an idol reign,
Creature of man's invention, ere this hap,
First shall the flesh be hacked from off my bones,
My bones be splintered as an icicle,
And every faculty within me bound
Submit to be called idiot, dotard, fool,
Fit dupe of kings, and kingly perfidy.

Enter EPHRAIM SAINTGOOD, *with military salute.*

Eph. Verily, I have sought thee long.

Crom. Well, Friend ?

Eph. Methinks the malignants have some plot a-foot.

Crom. Why thinkest thou that ?

Eph. I heard them boast that their captivity was
near its end ; and that they would now spoil the Egyp-
tians, their taskmasters.

Crom. When heardest thou this ?

Eph. Even at sunset, on the return from their
ungodly sport of hawking.

Crom. Thou hast well watched. Hast thou aught
else, friend ?

Eph. I have a message to thee, O General.

Crom. Unto me ? say on !

Eph. A wise child is better than a foolish father, and a general may learn wisdom even of a corporal.

Crom. Speak, friend ! as to a comrade speak !

Eph. General, it is written, Put not thy trust in princes, for there is no help in them : so then, I say ; I Ephraim Saintgood, a poor worker and a humble for the great cause, say to thee, Oliver Cromwell, who art our champion and a mighty man of valour, trust not this man ! Trust not Charles Stuart ; respect not persons : for he will bring back Baal, and the worshippers thereof.

Crom. Good ! Fail not, and faint not, Ephraim ! and, for the great births of providence now at hand, pray for me, that my faith fail not. The spirit is willing, but the flesh—thou knowest our poor weak flesh—it must be upheld, Ephraim, upheld. I say, then, pray for me ! pray without ceasing ! And yet once more, be watchful ! Keep thine ears open to hear, thine eyes to see. And if the malignants venture aught, even though it be Charles himself, thou hast a weapon, use it without fear. Enough ! Thy words shall be thought of.

Eph. Amen.   [*Exit.*

Iret. This news jumps with our fears : the advice is
    good.

Crom. He speaks but of surmise.

Iret.   Yet with surmising
Fancy is guide to reason.

Crom.   God will guide us
When His time comes.

Iret.   And is't not come?

Crom.   I know not.
His revelations linger. Ireton, come,

We'll to the King, propose our terms once more :
If he again refuse them——
    Iret.   Well, what then ?
    Crom. They shall not come again.
    Iret.   Thou art quite fixed ?
    Crom. I am.
    Iret.   This trial is the last ?
    Crom.   It is.
    Iret. And if, as well it may do, it too fail,
Thou wilt be firm ?
    Crom.   I will.   In God's good seasons
Come sometimes moments sent to try us, Ireton,
Yea, moments of pure gold.   If we do take them
With glad-eyed joy, and grateful humbleness,
They shower down bounties o'er us : all our lives
Transmuted by that sovereign alchemy,
Run of like metal, and, unmingled gold,
Make common earth as Heaven.   But if in pride,
Infatuate, dull of vision, we o'erlook
The shining chance ; if held in earthy dreams,
We view celestial treasuries outpour
Their stores unmoved ; then in just doom upon us
The Avenging Angel strikes the gift aside :
It will not come again.   Such is this time,
Which, ignorant of what a chance was here,
How rich, how fruitful (Pisgah's vision seen
Of glory, only to be forfeited),
Ages to come of unborn Englishmen
May execrating mourn.
    Iret.   He will reject it.
    Crom. Then on his head be all the consequence !
                                      [*Exeunt.*

ACT II.

SCENE I.—A ROOM IN HAMPTON COURT PALACE.

KING CHARLES *and* ASHBURNAM : *afterwards enter*
EPHRAIM SAINTGOOD, *who conceals himself.*

Ashb. (Reading a letter to the King.)   The Scotch
repent and see their error.

K. Charles.   Good !

Ashb.   The Parliament suspect the army.

K. Charles.   Good !

Ashb.   The army rages at the Parliament.

K. Charles. Good turns to better. See, all parties
join

To wish me back.   Where are my enemies ?

Ashb.   Fall'n, fall'n to bloody wrangling 'mong themselves.

K. Charles.   Have we been fighting shadows all this
time,

Like men in dreams, thinking them substances,

And wake to find the busy nightmare-fiend

Nought but a painted curtain ?

Ashb.   Good my Liege,

Give thy mirth rein !

K. Charles.   Ah, but some do not wake.

Across mine eye an apparition comes
Of some who still sleep on : some gory heads,
Some bleeding out of gashes in their sides,
Some clasping fettered hands, some shedding tears ;
And each of them as he goes shadowy by
Doth stop, and mutter vengeance. As I listen to them
Dark thoughts rise in me.

 Ashb.   Aye, a time shall come ;
Then, Cromwell, comes our turn (*aside*). Ha, see !

 K. Charles.   What is it ?

 Ashb. Cromwell ! I saw him as a blast go by :
He muttered as he went : his downcast eyes
Fixed, as there were some murder in his thought
Which he would hide : and once he clutched his sword,
Swaying, and full of passion as a sea,
Tossing with tempest.

 K. Charles. He is dangerous.

 Ashb. Leave him to me. I know a bait for him.

 K. Charles. What, for Leviathan himself?

 Ashb.   He follows
Tame as a dolphin, when I pipe of peace.

 K. Charles. O skilled Arion ! Yet—beware ! He
   stays not
On strict proprieties. What think you of him ?

 Ashb. Well, Sire, I think he is a hypocrite.

 K. Charles. That tells me nothing in the times we
   live in.
England is now so full of hypocrites,
And each of them so wondrous like the other,
That, by my soul, in all this godly flock
I can no more distinguish sheep from sheep,

      C 2

Without some brand to mark their difference.
Be more distinctive, friend !

    Ashb.   A hypocrite
But knowing not his own hypocrisy :
Ambitious, yet so politic he seems
To loathe ambition, to have greatness forced
Upon his shoulders, all too weak to bear it :
For so he feigns.   And then anon he'll weep,
Make protestations, sigh, and call to Heaven,
Swearing his simpleness, as though unsworn
No man would trust him : yet his word I doubt,
His oath I dread, and for his sighs and tears
I count them dregs of veriest falsity.

    K. Charles.   Say in a word, he is a Puritan.
Know one, know all !   After their sect they live
The strictest, straitest lovers of themselves
Earth ever looked on since the Pharisee.
They sin of pride, as others sin of pleasure,
And sin more grossly, being not in passion,
Nor tempted of hot blood ; but tyrant pride,
Herod-like, murders all their rising virtues,
Self-hating love, obedience, loyal fear,
Nature's sweet counterpoises to ambition :
And then, although Religion gilds the prow,
Profit, a wary pilot, takes the helm,
And steers them, (they as rowers, seated, turning
From that they strain for,) on into fair fortunes,
To riches, high advantage, golden gain :
Which as the snake, wily when hungering most,
Observed they will not touch, unseen suck down.
Oh ! better far one ounce of human love,

Though soft to weakness, than this sourest sin,
This stainless ice of cold hypocrisy.
   Ashb.   And will you trust such rogues?
   K. Charles.   I trust them?   Nay!
I will but use them for my purposes,
As they use me.
   Ashb.   Right!   Hold yourself aloof,
Biding the time; who gives the best of terms,
Extorting least, to him incline, but so
As to an enemy, with little trust
And less of love : the bitter pill of peace
Accepting as a brief but needful medicine,
For sickness wholesome, but with growing strength
Fit only to be spurned.   Thus hold yourself,
And soon all foes, Scotch, Army, Parliament,
Now by hard straining knit in fickle strands,
Slackened, shall as an illmade cord untwine,
The tug of war being over.
   K. Charles.   Good, this shall
Employ our thoughts.
   Eph. (apart.)   Good, this shall
Go to my lords.
   Ashb.   But we must keep this secret,
Close as a well, and darker than a mine,
Until the hour shall come for bursting it.
   K. Charles.   And then——
   Ashb.   And then shall these rebellious heads,
Whose high-aspiring greatness mocks the world,
Ascend yet higher : their bodies left behind
To fatten earth withal.
   K. Charles.   It will need skill.

Ashb.   That is the pleasure of it.   Leave all to me ;
If plotting be the air in which they breathe,
Plotting is my more native element.

Enter LORD DIGBY.

K. Charles.   Ha, my Lord Digby !

Digby (*presenting a letter on his knee*).   From her
    Majesty !

K. Charles.   A letter !   You have seen her ?   You
    have come
From her sweet presence ?

Digby.   With such speed, my Liege,
As man and horse can put into the hours
Of day and night, unresting.

K. Charles.   And she looked ?

Digby.   But sadly !

K. Charles.   They shall pay me for her tears.
But to her letter !   So, she writes me word—
' That she is weary of her banishment.
I must make peace.'   Said she aught else on this ?

Digby.   She would that you this peace might so con-
    sider
But as a truce and forging-time of war :
Not yielding, save the shadow and the name,
Keeping the substance.

K. Charles.   She would have me then
Keep the Militia ?

Digby.   Those her very words !

K. Charles.   And I will do it.   Quick, good Ash-
    burnham !
Give me a pen !   She shall have straight assurance

Of my strong will sooner to part with life
Than with the sword.   The name is not the King.
Better a rood of land, where I have power,
Than a whole realm with splendid impotence.

[*Writes : reads the last sentence aloud.*
' When the time comes I shall know very well how to
treat these rogues, and instead of a silken garter (which
is their daily prayer), I will fit them with a hempen
halter.'   Do you hear, Ashburnham ? a hempen halter !

Ashb.   All former proposals notwithstanding !

K. Charles.   Yes !   All former proposals notwith-
standing !
Now by a common boor this letter send,
Packed in a saddle, to the Boar in Holborn.
Our friends will do the rest.

Ashb.   I go, my Liege.

Eph.   The Boar in Holborn ? so !

[*Slips out, followed by* ASHBURNHAM, *and* LORD DIGBY.

K. Charles (Taking out a miniature).   Now let me
see herself.   Beautiful face !
The eye's dear love acquits the lip's light scorn,
Swearing it innocent.   So shines the sun
Above a bank of pouting April clouds,
To raise the drooped head of the violet,
And bid the storm-bound traveller, God speed !
Mark too that neck, whose pillared alabaster
Bears the chaste shrine above it with such pride,
As were no stain in angels.   Proud to serve,
Is humble to obey ; and sweeter shows
Love's freedom on a fond but equal brow,
Than slaves' idolatry.   O my sweet heart !

Present I love thee more than all the world,
Absent yet more.   This seems the truer life,
And all without mere shadows, and vain noise,
Aping reality.   If it be a dream,
It is a pleasant one, and I'll believe it,
Since pleasure comes so rarely.   Ha, who comes?

Enter CROMWELL *and* IRETON, *followed by* ASHBURNHAM.

 Iret.   We crave an audience, Sire.
 K. Charles.   Ye take it rather :
Using a gaoler's license, Generals.
 Iret.   It is no time to stand on ceremony :
We come on weighty business.
 K. Charles.   .   What is that ?
 Crom.   We bring the army's proffered terms once
  more.
 K. Charles.   Those I have once rejected ?
 Crom.   Sire, the same ?
 K. Charles.   As ?
 Crom.   The surrender to the Commissioners
Of the Militia.
 K. Charles.   Never.
 Crom.   For ten years,
 K. Charles.   By God, not for an hour.
 Crom.   .   Yet, Sire, bethink you,
Less cannot well content victorious men.
 K. Charles.   Less cannot ? then beshrew me, ask for
  more !   . .
And then grow humble with defeat again ;
. For less or more is all too much for me.
 Crom.   We ask it in the name o' the common good.

K. Charles. The common good! I hate that common good,
When not a word is said of loyalty.
Yet stay: if I accept these goodly terms,
What will ye do?
  Iret.   Replace you on your throne!
  Crom. And place that throne upon a people's love,
Diviner right than all the boast of kings.
  K. Charles. My people's love? O shallow! Bid again:
Bid mountains higher! for if words be aught,
And pledges hold, my people's love is mine:
And who so fond and lavish that would buy
What is his own? Nay, sirs, ye wrong my subjects:
They fight me, true; but 'tis to show their zeal:
Enrol battalions, still 'tis in my name:
Use my revenues, but to do me good:
And so they love me doubtless, though they hate
The things I love: and they would have me King,
Though with no atom of a kingly rule;
But keep me as a robe of ceremony,
To grace high courts, and solemn festal shows,
Or use my name as covering to the world,
To cloak self-seeking pranks of villainy.
  Crom. We should betray our cause with less than this.
  K. Charles. Who made that cause, and who made
  you to make it?
The Parliament from which ye now rebel.
  Iret. We came not here to bandy idle words.
  K. Charles. Was it the Spirit moved you to speak
  thus?
  Crom. It is the army's cause.

K. Charles.   Who cares for that?

Crom.   I know a man would give his life for it.

K. Charles.   Ye love not peace who proffer terms
   like these.

Crom.   Without them peace were quickly war again.

Iret.   Take these, or none !

K. Charles.   Sir !

Iret.   These, I say, or none !

K. Charles.   And wherefore? But to make of rebels
   kings?

Of kings, the servants of rebellious vassals?

And out of England's ruin——

Iret.   To rebuild

A better England !

K. Charles.   Babel-building all,

Whose builders, working in despite of Heaven,

Already see their towering dream dissolve

Mid strife of tongues.   Ye do not know your weakness,

Nor where your strength is.   Felt ye but your needs,

Ye would entreat my pardon : ye would come

In sackcloth, pale, with ashes on your heads,

And pray me to return : Ye would go barefoot,

Live all your days as in a cemetery,

With eyes for mourners, heavy hearts for graves,

And, next to your Salvation, pray to be

Delivered from dissension.   Oh I see

Rebellion's sickness : 'tis a teeming snake

Whose brood devour the womb from which they sprung :

A flame consuming all things, last itself :

A hideous deep that holds all other deeps,

A hundred deeps in one.   I could run on——

                    [*Rises and walks about.*

Iret. What does he mean?

Ashb.   Be patient, and in time
Himself will tell you.

K. Charles.   The worst punishment
That can a nation for its guilt befall,
Is when its King says, he will reign no more.

Iret. (to Crom.) Let us begone!

[*Crom. signs to him to be still.*

K. Charles. I am the peace of England,
And in me outcast ye have banished peace,
That but with me will never more return.
Ye misproud men, ye know not where ye stand;
Ye bid me to remember things of earth,
The chance of arms, the treacherous accident
Of freakish war. But I bid you remember
Far higher things, that have their source in Heaven—
The holy altar, the anointing balm,
The laying on of consecrated hands,
The intercession calling blessing down,
And all that went to mark and make me King.
Can such things be, yet leave us as before?
Ah, no! it was no mortal sanction, Cromwell,
Gave me the power: from God Himself it came :
And God alone can take it from my hands,
And unto God I turn me for revenge.   [*Exit.*

Iret. What does he mean?

Crom.   Explain this sudden mood.
Came we as borrowers, or as lenders here?

Ashb. He who can presage all the inconstant wind,
Or reckon up the voices of the noon,
Map out the mazes of the rivulet,

Or count the clouds that fleck an April sky,
He can explain the humours of the mind.

Iret. This is no answer to our question, Sir.

Ashb. They are as freakish as the ape itself,
As many as our faculties : a dream,
A passing hope, a fancy, a surprise,
May all beget them ; or a twitching nerve,
An ill digestion, or a showery day.

Crom. Have done, Sir, with this fooling, and begone!

Ashb. Why look you there ! I call Philosophy
To make you answer, and you call me fool.

              [IRETON *stamps impatiently.*

Aye stamp, and call the Devil to your aid !
Whene'er you need him, he is always nigh.

Iret. What did the King mean when he called us
    weak,
Doomed without him to fall?

Ashb.   Did he say so?
Why then to-morrow he will like enough
Unsay it : such is man's consistency.
Adieu, my Lords, I leave you to yourselves.

              [*Exit, humming an Air.*

    With a hah, hah, hah, and a hey, hey, ho,
    As down the stream we merrily go.

Crom. Fools, madmen, moping drivellers that they
    are !
Wide-gaping idiots round the juggler's throne !
As Pharaoh blinded, even when the surge
Gathered to drown him.

Iret.   And as impotent !

Crom. O England !·that such men should govern
thee !

What think you of all this ?

Iret.   'Tis Hampton Court.

Crom. I do not mean the place.

Iret.   By Wolsey built.

Crom. Are you too mad ?

Iret.   No, but most sensible
That the real madness is to forfeit friends,
Yet win not a foe's love. So Wolsey fell,
With but one Cromwell still his friend to serve him,
By giving to King Henry more than God.

Enter EPHRAIM SAINTGOOD.

Crom. What, Ephraim, again? so soon ? Has aught
happened?

Eph. Truly, yes, O General !

Iret. Then truly tell it, and with haste, hearest
thou ?   (*Shaking him.*)

Eph. In sooth——

Iret. In sooth thou art a fool.

Eph. I was in the inner chamber, hidden amid the
stuff, like the young man Saul——

Iret. Oh ! the plague on all similitudes ! Quick ! to
thy story's point, man !

Eph. When lo ! there entered in the man, the man
Charles Stuart, with him they call Ashburnham : and
after divers considerations between them, with little
grace——

Iret. Oh !

Eph. And little fitting for thine ears to hear,
General.

Crom.   They spoke ill of me : they hate me : I know it, Ephraim, I know it ; but proceed !

Eph.   They came at last to the writing of a letter to the wicked woman Jezebel, even to the Queen ; which letter, full of evil matter and dangerous, will be sent erenight by the bearing of a poor man's shoulders, packed in a saddle, to the Boar in Holborn.

Crom.   To the Queen !

Iret.   To the archplotter, the mother of all mischief, the stirrer-up of war, the enemy of peace !

Crom.   The child of him, who sold his God, his religion for a crown !   It is the clue, Ireton : it is the clue.   Disguises quick !   God has sent this witness to us.   That letter shall be ours ere we sleep.   Quick, Ireton !   Oh ! we will be all action now.   No more delay, but action, action, action !   Quick !   In that letter lies England's fortune : do you hear me ?   England's life and fortune, and—her King's.   [*Exeunt.*

SCENE II.—COUNCIL CHAMBER.

KING CHARLES, ORMOND, ASHBURNHAM, BERKELEY.

K. Charles.   What yield to them ?   Does Ormond
        counsel yield ?
Nay then be stubborn, O my wavering soul !
Thy reasons ?

Orm.   These, our coffers all are empty,
Our armies perished, and true cavaliers
Grown hopeless ; (happier they who fell in battle,

'Scaped from despair !) though should their Master call
 them,
To a man they will as gaily mount the block
As ever on grey morn they mounted steed,
And halloed ' tantivy ' to the western wind,
When the good pack's sweet music cheered the field.
 K. Charles.   I have no words : thou answer, Ash-
 burnham.
 Ashb.   Nay, my good Lord, permit me, by your leave !
These things must not be judged by the outer eye :
Much is that seems not, much that is not seems.
And herein lies our politician's art,
Twixt two opposing currents of like seeming,
To know the difference betwixt ' is ' and ' seems.'
 Orm.   And in this art you are a master, Sir ?
 Ashb.   I am.   When yet, a simple boy at school,
I ever loved to fish the troubled stream,
Leaving the smooth to one who was my friend,
Whence, lazy, he would draw the sluggish bream ;
He afterwards became an Alderman.
 Orm.   Prythee, the point !
 Ashb.   The point, my lord, is coming.
 Orm.   And so is Doomsday.   [*Aside.*
 Ashb.   .   But the handle first ;
He who would take a sword up by the point
Must look to cut his fingers.
 Orm.   Well, proceed !
 Ashb.   So then, in short, we have our secret ground,
(Which being yet to build on must be secret)
To deem our Cause, seeming dejected, hopeless,

Never more high, more hopeful, since the day
Our banner first was raised at Nottingham.

    Orm. How?

    Ashb. And what valour ruined in the field,
That will we of the Chamber soon restore
By nicer arts of healing management.

    Orm. By management? Oh for a housewife's broom
To brush these mouldy cobwebs from thy brain !
(*To K. Charles.*) Beware of trifling, Sire, with bearded
    men,
Whose wits are keener, curse them, than their swords.

    K. Charles. What, Ormond, doubt the goodness of
    our Cause?

    Orm. I fear 'tis hopeless.

    K. Charles.   Ah ! that word again !
Nothing is hopeless but a hopeless man.

    Orm. Blind beggar'd hope needs wisdom's leading
    string.

    Ashb. Even in hell the devils scorn despair.

    Orm. What devil was it bade thee counsel thus?

    Ashb. What angel taught thee to oppose a King?

    K. Charles. Nay, Ormond, if thou lovest me, grudge
    me not
The beggar's wealth, bright hope of better things.

    Orm. If I do love thee, O my royal Master !

    K. Charles. Why then doth my entreaty vainly
    plead?

    Orm. Must then this bleeding England bleed again?
Widows fulfil their tears, mothers their moans,
Sons follow fathers to the monuments
That scarce have sealed up their sculptured stones,

And all which has been, be to that shall be,
The dreary prelude to a tragic tale,
Grief's crimson'd picture not its bloodier self?
Think of war's woes!

   K. Charles.   Who feels them more than I?

   Orm. The joys of peace!

   K. Charles.   I have them all by heart,
Glib as a lover has his mistress' charms;
Who dotes on her perfections, yet for duty
Flees 'them.

   Orm. And may I hear the number of them?
Perchance when urged into another's ear,
They will in very urging grow more sweet,
Than reckoned o'er in listless solitude.

   K. Charles. A thousand times! As thus—O what a
      thing .
To have the power to end all with one word!
To send the soldier home to plough his field,
Yoking his bony charger to the team:
To bid the glad bells ring, the ale-cask flow:
To lead rich Plenty back, with buxom Peace,
And troops of laughing children round their knees:
Sweetly to join long-sunder'd families:
To reconcile the country with the town:
And through the length and breadth of merry England
Rekindle hearths quenched by these piteous wars:
When all these joys rest but on one small word,
Was ever tyrant so ungentle born,
So hard, so loveless, misanthropical,
As not to say that word?

   Orm.   Oh say it, say it!

K. Charles. Did I hear 'say it,' Ormond counsel
  ' say it ' ?

Orm. Can my liege answer arguments like these
Drawn by himself?

K. Charles.   These are no arguments,
But tender pictures for a lady's chamber,
Whose eye is all her conscience : sterner men,
God's nobler image, owning laws of duty,
Are moved but in the soul.

Orm.   May I hear reasons?

K. Charles. And is there any need to tell to Ormond
The feelings of a King?   Shall I give up
Because Rebellion weds the strumpet Fortune,
Which now is his, now mine, now any man's,
Who stoops to woo her ; shall I render up
My patrimony, the birthright of my heirs,
From unremembered ages handed down,
My heaven-appointed trust, my right divine,
(Never more needed than in times like these,)
And live a pageant's show, a puppet-king,
A name, a crown, a purple robe, no more?
Or shall I, false to holy Church, God's flock,
Break down its walls, drive out its sacred pastors,
A government far older than my own,
And leave it to the bear, the fox, the wolf;
I on whose shoulders lies an oath to guard it,
And so to keep a kingdom, lose a soul?
Name it not, Ormond.   Am I the less a man,
Being a King, to fear to answer, Nay,
As I see cause, which freedom is not grudged
To the most abject?   Or shall I attaint

Those loving, true, those almost matchless men,
Who fought for me, their sole crime loyalty,
That is, their duty ?   Never fear it, Falkland !
I will not wrong thy unstained memory.
Still art thou unconvinced ? 'Wouldst have me still,
Thou spotless flower of old nobility,
Even for peace, chief blessing temporal,
Give up the eternal blessing held in store
For those who keep their truth firm to the end ?
No, that thou wouldst not, I can see thou wouldst not ;
Thou dost not come of such a stock as that.

    Orm.   I melt : my bosom as a furnace burns,
Fired with thy words.
    K. Charles.   I knew it would, dear friend.
    Orm.   Give but the word, and we will bleed again,
(He is a rebel who refuses it),
Bleed our last drop, and call that drop a laggard
That flows the last : then dying, our last words
Shall leave the bloody quarrel to our heirs,
Entailing it a legacy for ever,
Sooner than see our master lose his right,
Sooner than budge a single inch from honour.
    K. Charles.   There spoke—what jargon to this
        peddling age !
The great old heart of glorious chivalry.
To Ireland then, and raise my banner high,
Inviting all who love me to revolt !
My blessing go with thee (*raising Ormond who kneels*),
        not there but here,
Here on my heart, thou peerless Englishman !
That height alone is level with thy worth.

Farewell, farewell (*Exit Ormond*); if all were such as he,
Earth would return to Paradise. Come, friend! [*Exeunt.*

SCENE III.—BLUE BOAR, HOLBORN.

LANDLORD *and* WIFE.

Land. (*sings*).

> He and she could not agree.
>   It was sultry weather :
> He would pant with the window wide,
> She would freeze at the very fireside :
>   They could not live together.

Well, dame Margery, what's the matter now?

Mar. Something's going to happen, or my name's
not Margery. It's not for nothing that the soot came
down the chimney this blessed night, and the new flitch
of bacon, that was bought of goodman Hardacre a year
ago come next Michaelmas, fell down off its hook in the
best parlour, and upset the table, and frightened the cat,
and woke me out of as sweet and pleasant a slumber as
ever a young maid had on St. Agnes' eve. It's not for
nothing, I say——

Land. Stop that, wife! stop that! You'll bring the
house as well as the soot about our ears with that tongue
of yours. Bring me a can of beer, I say, and be quick
about it!

> He and she could not agree.
>   It was wintry weather :
> He with a single sheet would lie,
> She would pile the blankets high :
>   They could not sleep together.

Now wife, have you got that beer?

Mar. No, and I'm not a-going to get it neither, not
if I die for it!

Land. Die for it! Hum!

> He and she could not agree.
> It was sickly weather :
> She fell ill, and to heaven would go,
> Bid him follow—He said, No, No !
> We should make hell together.

But who's that (*a knocking*) at such an hour of night?
Again! again! Coming, coming! Lord, what a hurry
some folk are in!

Enter CROMWELL *and* IRETON *disguised, followed by*
RICHARD *bearing a saddle.*

Crom. Come, host, a strong quart of Martinmas ale
for this poor fellow! and then, sirrah, we would be alone.
Go you and mind your horse in the stable, and we'll dry
your saddle by the fireside. 'Tis a stormy night.

Rich. Noa. I were tould not to part wi' saddle to
any man.

Land. (*with beer*). Come, here's as good a mug of
beer as ever old Noll himself brewed at Huntingdon.

Crom. Let me have a taste of it. (*Drinks.*) Nay,
he'd brew better beer than that, I can tell you.

Land. What do you know about it?

Crom. Know? Oh, I know he would: and teach·
you better too, my little host, I'll be his warranty (*pinch-
ing his ear playfully*) for that. But here, fellow, take
your beer; and now go. I'll take care of your saddle for
you (*taking it*).

Rich. I were tould not to part wi' saddle to any man.

Crom. Do as I tell you, sirrah, and make haste.

Rich. Oh dear, dear, dear! Well, you will be obeyed, I see. Take care of it, gentlemen. Now, sir (*to the landlord*), will you show a poor fellow the way?

[*Exeunt.*

Crom. And now, dame, get us your back parlour ready, and set a light there. We have business anon. Quick!

Mar. Well, lawkaday, what a man he is! He makes me feel all of a twitter like, as if I'd an aguy-fit, which, God save us all, I had last Christmas in the great frost, when the milk froze the pails, and——

Crom. Come, good lady, come——

Mar. Going, sir, going!   [*Exit.*

(CROMWELL *and* IRETON *tear open the saddle, find the letter, and make all right just as* RICHARD *returns.*)

Rich. Now, if that saddle——

Iret. Here's your saddle, good fellow, and good-night to you. We're going into the next room. [*Exeunt.*

Rich. Well, if anyone had said to me, Richard—that's my name—Richard, you'll part with that saddle to any man afore night, I'd have said he was a liar. (*Drinks.*) But there's the saddle, d——e, and here I am. I know when a man can be trusted, and when he can't. There's some as can't see a hole in a ladder, and some as can see through a brick wall. Leave me alone for that! (*Drinks.*) And that fellow Bill Baker said as I had no more brains than a turnip, and were only fit to scare pigeons off farmers' peaas. But they didn't choose 'im

fur this job. Noa, they choase me. Here, Mr. Landlord, show me the way to bed, will you ? (*Looks vacantly
at the mug.*)   Well, it's strange as looking at that ere mug
makes a fellow so dizzy-like. I'd a sworn now there were
two mugs there. Well, now a-feel sleepy, and 'ull go to
bed. This talking so much a-nights ain't wholesome.

    Land. Come along with me, Richard; I'll give you
a bed as soft as buttercups, and as sweet as new-mown
hay, to lie on.

    Rich. Well, I'll gi' you a stave afore I go.   [*Sings.*

Now Buttercup was a good milch-cow,
   But she would not stand the pail :
So the maid tripped here, and the maid tripped there,
   And the maid tripped down the dale.

But Ladybird was another sort,
   As steady as any nail :
Yet the maid tripped here, and the maid tripped there,
   And the maid tripped down the dale.

Now then, master, the light this a'way ! I didn't ask
you for two lights now. Come along ! [*Exit, with saddle.*

    CROMWELL *and* IRETON *return reading letter.*[2]

    Iret. ' Dear heart, my cause looks better than it has
done for many a long day. I am courted by both
factions, and shall join that whose conditions are most to
my advantage. For the present I am more minded to
treat with the Scotch than with the army. For the rest,
I alone understand my position: be quite easy as to the
conditions which I may grant. When the time comes, I
shall very well know how to treat these rogues, and,

       [2] See Appendix.

instead of a silken garter (which is their daily prayer), I
will fit them with a hempen halter.'

    Crom. Could this have been believed?

    Iret.   My true suspicions!

    Crom. Fine tricks to mock his God with!

    Iret.   He, the flower
Of knighthood, fount of honour in his realm! ··

    Crom. Read it again.   [*He reads it.*

    Iret.   Oh, surely it were well
To mend our English manners, and turn Scotch,
Better than hang!

    Crom.   No, by the eternal God,
These cross and tangled ways have but one end— ·
Their own confusion.

    Iret.   Worthy Ashburnham,
Methinks I read in this thy cunning hand:
A hempen halter! Good! most witty phrase!
Oh, I could laugh!

    Crom.   So much for policy!
Away with it to the hell where doubters lie,
And every 'but' and 'if' in all the world.

    Iret. What shall we do?

    Crom.   Ne'er trust Charles Stuart more.

    Iret. With my consent we ne'er had trusted him.

    Crom. I would trust all, till fully proven false.

    Iret. And I trust none save who are proven true.
But what to do? I like not to advance,
Save on a certain path to a clear goal.

    Crom. What shall we do? Nay, that is policy;
To chart the ocean, and map out the sky
In parcels, like to cunning mariners.

We sail upon a sea, whose secret slumbers
Fathoms below invention's deepest line.
Beneath our undiscovered starless skies
Prediction wanders silent.   God will steer us.
I do believe that God himself will come
Visible to a thousand straining hearts,
And in the dark eclipse of reason shine
To guide true souls that trust Him.
    Iret.   Dost thou mean——
    Crom.   I do mean nothing.
    Iret.   Think then what thou wilt,
And call it nothing: give thy thought no name
Until the birth : yet let not names affright thee :
We at whose deeds the world doth stand amazed
Should tremble not at names.   Yet one more word !
Do what thou wilt of new and fearful, Cromwell ;
I will not shrink to follow.   Count on me !   [*Exit.*
    Crom. (*Crumpling up the letter.*)   ' The King can do
    no wrong.'   Vile sophistry !
I know a saying worth this ten times over :
' Put not your trust in princes,' that is true,
Though 'twas no servile lawyer uttered it.
              (*A pause ; then passionately.*)
So he will have it, War, unpitying War ;
No parleying and no quarter.   Be it so !
I take his choice ; our Arbiter be War !
Yet dread it, Charles !   I am not one of those
Content with halfness, timorous shrinking back
(As one who finds a lion in his snare),
From my own victory.   When I draw the sword,
True to my God, though rebel to my king,

I know no fear but not to do enough
For Him I follow.   'Twixt the first starting-point
And the last consummation, goal of all,
Lies there for me no halt, no resting-place :
Unswerving as a bolt I go right on :
And if some miserable child of man
Stand in my path, stand 'twixt me and my Cause,
Then by the God who made that Cause and me,
Chose me His Captain, gave me His revenge,
Sent me His death-dispensing minister,
Though he my very friend were, son, or brother,
I'd stamp him into powder.   King, beware !   [*Exit.*

ACT III.

SCENE I.—IN FRONT OF WINDSOR CASTLE.

Soldiers and people on the terrace; the KING *passes into the Castle.*

Woman (with child in her arms). Well I say, bless the King! let who will wag his tongue against me.

Man. Hush! dame, hush! you'll get us all into trouble.

Woman. Then go home, and a wanion light on you for a cuckoldy knave and coward! Hush! Don't you hush me! hush your own wife, neighbour Rumsey. Aye, we know who's got the shrill voice at home. I say, God bless his Majesty.

Several. And so say I, and I, &c.

Wom. And much good have all these wranglings and fightings done us. Why there's never a lad may wear a loveknot in his sleeve, or see a pair of game-cocks ruffle each other's feathers, or toss a pot, or kiss a lass, but he must go before a magistrate. The devil fly away with all Roundheads! Let's have the good old times back again.

1st Presbyterian. Yes; the good old times with a penny to pay to courtier this, and courtier that, for every pound of salt, or pat of butter, you bought at fair or market! I'm not for being hard on the poor King now he's down : but I'm not for the good old times.

2nd Presbyterian. Aye, and not a glass of beer to be had, or a herring to be hung in the chimney corner, but it must pay toll to some rogue in silk or violet, who would spend it all on his filfthy queans up in London yonder!

Wom. Well, and if he did, he spent it all openly and as a gentleman, which is more than these sneaking rascals do. Aye, who killed the good hen for laying an egg on Sunday, and then paid poor blind Giles his wages in bad halfpennies?

Sold. Take care, mistress, or you'll have a chance of the cucking stool.

Wom. Take care! who'll make me take care? Aye, you're brave enough against women : but if we had good Prince Rupert here with a score of cavaliers, he'd swinge a hundred such as you from here to Oxford.

Sold. Come, dame.

Wom. Ah, I know you, I know you. You're just as bad as they were, only you do it secretly. There's many a pretty lass in Windsor could tell a tale, an' she would. Tush, we'd the devil in scarlet once, with a feather in his cap, and now we've the devil in grey.

Man. Come, adone with this, wife ; have done ! What an' if it be the devil, it's no use telling him so. Go home with you, go home. I'm not going to lose my ears for your folly.

Wom. Nay, keep them, donkey'! to match your braying! Go home indeed! Aye, I'll go home with some brave boy who'll fear nothing for his Church and

King. Oh bless his Majesty ! See, here· he comes himself.

        [*The King comes forward, and they retire*
          without being seen.

K. Charles. 'Twas here I brought her when our
   hearts were young,
The summer-birds sang greeting, and the bells
Rang as they would shake welcome out of stone,
Like music from old Memnon. On through flowers
We floated, like to creatures of the air,
Bright gossamers that drink the morning dews,
And net the sunbeams. Life flowed all in love,
And love too full ran over, now in tears,
And now in laughter, pleasure tipped with pain,
Yet pain itself sweet pleasure. Happiest time,
That knew not it was happy ! Oh how changed,
How is all changed ! The summer sun is gone :
Withered the roses hang upon the wall :
The birds sit mute : the bells for others ring :
And she, my Queen, my love, for whom all this
Was all too little, joyless wife, or widow
All but in name, leads banished hopeless days :
And I, whom many countries call their king,
Pass through my kingdoms like a thief at night,
And early-ageing look but for a grave,
Goal of sad cares, and long captivity.
     [*Girls come forward and bring a nosegay for the King.*
     K. Charles. Roses still left ! and friends not wholly
       gone !
Strange commentary on my text of woe !
       [*The people come out, and salute the King with cries*
         of ' God save your Majesty !'

K. Charles. Well met, dear friends, dearer that all is
　　gone
Beside you !　'Mid the ruin that has swept
Over my life, the general wrack of all,
Your love for me, a little Ararat
Amid a deluge, still unshaken stands,
And recks not of the unbitted raging storm,
That drowns the world in floods of enmity.
　　　　　[*They press round to kiss his hands, then woman*
　　　　　　holding up her child says ' Touch him for the
　　　　　　evil, Your Majesty !'
　　K. Charles. The　evil !³　Aye, there's virtue in　me
　　still :
It flows in me, it courses in my veins ;
And poor as is the temple of this body,]
Yet in it dwells a spirit so divine,
No treason can unthrone its sovereignty.
　　　　　　　　　　　[*Touches it; then people retire.*
　　K. Charles. Old towers and halls, time-honoured seat
　　of kings,
And ye o'erfrowning and embattled fronts,
Grey with the hoary rime of centuries,
Do I again salute you ?　Open wide
Your ancient doors, and whence once issued forth
Fresh as the morning, bright with morning's beam,
An Edward's might, a Margaret's haughty smile,
The pomp of Henry splendidly attired,
While Surrey, Suffolk, Bohun, round him thronged,
And Wolsey bent for once the aspiring knee,
Now welcome single back a captive king !

　　　　　　　³ See Appendix.

Poor, friendless, vanquished, king in name alone,
The substance gone to enrich my enemies.
Yet, O my Sires, where'er ye reign in bliss,
Canonized Saints, heroic royal shades,
Plantagenet and Tudor, greet your Son,
Who evil-fortuned, not degenerate,
Now asks your aid! If of my sacred trust
In coward fear or weakness I have aught
Betrayed, aught lightly perill'd, or wronged my throne,
Loving soft ease, or pride, or wanton pleasure,
More than my duty, let these men do all!
For my soul's sin let my poor life atone,
And pity write my pardon in the grave!
But if, as though at some great trumpet call
Startling from slumber, if for God and truth
I still have battled, ready to bear all,
All, toil, want, suffering, worst of ignominy,
Ready to suffer, only not to reign,
Most despicable, a puppet, not a king:
False to myself, my sons, and you, my sires:
Then rescue me, though not with fleshly arms,
Nor with war's weapons: plant in treacherous hearts,
Plant once again the germ of blessed peace:
And, whence ye watch the waxing and the wane
Of human things, shed on it heavenly dews,
Till a waste land blossom and smile once more.   [*Exit.*

SCENE II.—TAVERN NEAR WESTMINSTER.

LANDLORD *with jolly face, but shaven : takes a cavalier wig out of a drawer, and tries it on.*

Land. Lord, that an honest man should have to wear three faces! for the King one, and for the Army one, and for the Parliament one! three men in one! and that this should be liberty. Curse me liberty, say I. When we had no liberty, a man might be that he would; drain his glass, love his wench, and dress in taffeta or fustian according to his liking. Now every one will shape you after their liking. Is it John Presbyter who comes? Mine host, quoth he, methinks thy wine is vinegar. Vinegar forsooth ! The devil take them all for sour, fault-finding, hole-picking knaves ! And yet drat 'em, they know what good liquor is, and they'll have it too. And your soldier, your accursed Ironside, who will break your head, an' you praise not Oliver, and defame the King ! And your cavalier, who will drink tenfold to drown care, and pay you nought but promises, or love-tokens, because of the bad times ! And this is liberty ! Ah, for the good old days, when a man wore his long love-locks as nature made him. Now men are nought but shorn apes, chattering the more that they may seem wise. Come, I will refurnish my head with hair. (*Puts on a cavalier wig.*) There, cursed Round-head, thou art as God made thee. (*Draws rapier.*) Sa, Sa! La, La! (*Swaggers and lunges.*) Come, gentlemen, the King's health, God bless him! No shirking there ! Bumpers all! Here's to the last sigh

of the last Roundhead in England ! Aha, now I'll thank
you for a stave. (*Sings.*)

> So here's to the health of our noble King Charles !
> And here's to the bonny Queen Mary !
> To hell with the Roundhead, who cavils and snarls,
> And all who of liquor are chary !

> Rollicking boys, rollicking boys,
> Make the roof echo with laughter and noise !
> Drink it in cyder, and drink it in sack !
> Crash the glass, smash the glass, over your back !

.   [*Doing it.*
(*A knock.*)   The devil ! Who knocks ? (*Listens.*) 'Tis
a sober knock : that is no cavalier. Off curls ! 'Tis a
grave knock, that is no Ironside. Now face, thy sourest
look ! Come in, Sirs, come in !   [*Opens the door.*

Enter the EARL *of* DENBIGH, IRETON, LAMBERT, LUDLOW,
   HUTCHINSON, HARRISON, *and various leaders of Inde-*
   pendents.

The devil ! Your most obedient, your worships' most
obedient. What is your wish, gentlemen ?

   Iret. Bring us what you will, and speedily : nay,
leave us what is there already. We come not for drinking. And begone. Here is money for you.

                                             [*Exit* LANDLORD.

   Ld. D. Attaint the King, my masters, are ye mad ?
   Iret. Prythee, why mad ?
   Ld. D.   In his name laws do run,
Courts have their session, Judges their high place,
And from him only treason hath a name.
   Iret. If he offend——
   Ld. D.   Offend ? It is a question

E

Of treason and of death. Oh, had you seen him
At Newport, there, when the Commissioners
Pressed him so hard, twixt Pride and Sorrow seated,
His two advisers, now as memory urged him
Insisting on his right, then, wiser-prompted,
Withdrawing with a sigh : hopeless yet hoping :
The while he seemed with sad and patient smile
To welcome in changed fortunes : had you seen him,
Like a true gentleman, thus mild and noble,
Life-weary, yet his all of life remaining
Bent not to tarnish, bent to live in honour,
Over rebellious grief ruling a king,
In nothing less than royal : had you seen this,
And not been made of marble, you had wept
As certainly as we did.

  Iret.   And our tears,
Like spendthrift and unthinking prodigals,
Had wept away our freedom. So once more
I say, if he offend——

  Ld. D.   Offending perish !

  Iret. Then perish also law !

  Ld. D.   Nay, you show law !
Where is your precedent, your pattern framed
For such strange course?

   · *Lamb.*   What need of precedent?
We that have ventured on these brand-new ways
Must rather make than search for precedent.

  Ld. D. Yet, ere it be too late, good Sirs, bethink you,
How ye do shake by haste precipitate
The fair conditions of our ancient State
That stand all in the King ! The State's an Arch,

Built slowly up by many a cunning builder,
Sagacious spirits, wisest in our land.
Religion lies the deep foundation-stone :
Peace guards the corner : Law directs the plan :
While riches, honour, learning, noble birth,
Add each a stage, for use or ornament,
And justice keeps proportion in the whole.
Yet still the great Arch stands not.   It doth hang
Imperfect, scaffolded, and boarded up,
Like to a strong man palsied, propped on crutches,
Itself in contradiction to itself,
Till dropped from Heaven the royal keystone fall,
The King's great name.   Then as a thing of life,
Spanning Time's torrent with a lordly bound,
It bends and bears the world upon its back,
A glory and a marvel.   Yet this work
Ye would destroy.   Rash men, ye would unloose,
(That harmony, that ruling power withdrawn,)
The jar of opposites, setting faction free,
With adverse tyrannies to o'errun the world.

    Lud.   My Lord, your heat o'ercomes you : we are men
Can feel as you, can reason well as you——

    Ld. D.   But ye are blind, misguided, cannot see
The impending ruin.   Take away the King,
And straight ye bring destruction on your fields,
Let havoc loose, sink peace, mar everything.

    Lamb.   My Lord, you waste your breath.   If the
     King die,
I say but if——

    Ld. D.   If, and a willing mind,
Soon jump together.   Be advised ! be warned !

Be just, not cruel ! Such a crime will taint
E'en our good deeds, the first deeds done so well.
Oh ! we that drew the sword 'gainst tyranny,
Let us not end in tyranny ourselves.

Iret. Enough of this ! Declare your party, Lord !
Take part with us, or——

Ld. D.　　　　　　　　I take part with you !
Forbid it, Heaven ! take part with cannibals !
Alas ! I did but think to lop abuse,
Prune down exuberant and growing power ;
Till justice should, as sunshine, creeping in
Warm the pale shoots, earth's humbler stock below.
And lo ! I have put the axe in bloody hands
Of levellers, whose fell unpitying rage
Would hew down trunk and all.　　　　[*Rushes out,*

Iret.　　　　　　　So get you gone !
And every squeamish stomach in the land
That danger sickens ! If the great forget
Their duty's post, then forward humbler men !
What say you, Sirs ? the settlement of England,
For which we strove, seems farther than before.
What is the cause ?

Several.　　　The King.

Iret.　　　　　　　'This bleeding land
Is an Aceldama, a place of blood.
What is the cause ?

Several.　　　The King.

Iret.　　　　　　　Who roused the Scotch
To ravage England ? Who by Ormond's hand
In Ireland lit rebellion ?

Several.　　　Still the King !

Iret. Why, then, go to ! Were he a common man,
As you or I, this were not left to be
Not for an instant. Had he as many lives
As he has hairs, and for each mortal hair
A monarch's crown, they all were forfeited.
And wherefore have we fought and shed our blood,
If not to prove that kings are common men,
Thrones but gilt boards, and sceptres ivory wands,
As prelates' mitres coverings for the head,
All else mere drivelling, and doters' dreams,
The schemer's art, the fool's idolatry ?

Hutch. Why waste we words? The man of blood
must die.

Lamb. Must die?

Hutch.   Must die ! His office is the cause
Whence come our sufferings. Israel asked a King,
Which God, rejected, in His anger gave them :
That was the great Rebellion ; then did man,
The single light of all the world extinguished,
Left to himself go darkly groping on,
And soil his steps through miry accidents.
O friends, dear friends, the great revolt was there :
And these our wars come as rebuking plagues
To bid us on our knees to Him return,
Our lawful King, renew old vows to Heaven,
And, through rebellion ceasing to rebel,
Apostate once destroy apostacy.

Lud. Prythee decide ! we dally. 'Tis no time
To mince fine words. Why have a king at all ?
We were born equal : equal do we grow:
Arrive at equal stature. We are made

All of one paste, one substance.   In our veins
Do course like passions.   Wherefore then uprear
One man upon our shoulders, call him King,
Flatter and cringe to him, till he come to think
That he was born taller than other men?
Were it my choice, I would brook no man's rule,
Not even of my own father.

    Lamb.   Liberty
Be now henceforth our only Sovereign !
'Till it be known, Kings are not better men,
As being Kings, though to a sceptre born :
But should be chosen Kings, as better men.

    Lud. Yet we forget.   What says the General
To this our policy?

    Hutch.   What General?
Fairfax or Cromwell?

    Iret.   Do we need a name,
A scrape of ink to fill a parchment up,
A leaden seal to put upon a bond,
An attestation to an inventory,
Then I say, Fairfax.   Tush ! you know the men :
Fairfax to Cromwell, 'tis Minerva's owl
Against Minerva : Vulcan to Jupiter :
A dull-browed Ajax to the God of war.
What you would say about the General,
That say of Cromwell.

    Hutch.   Nay, the other's brave :
A valiant captain, tried and apt to war.
You do injustice.

    Iret.   .   Brave, but no more wit
Where deep-laid dangers deeper counsel need,

And stratagem must cope with stratagem,
Than his paid drummer ! while (in reverence)
To speak of Cromwell, not disparage him,
Needs men of stuff like Cromwell.
    Hutch.   I distrust him.
    Iret. . .You know him not.
    Hutch.   None know him : scarce, I think,
He knows himself.
    Iret.   There is he like to you,
Like me, like all, like to the times we live in :
Where young to-morrow laughs at old to-day,
Calling its wisdom out of date and stale,
Forgotten like a last year's almanack.
    Hutch.   I like not this.   Beware !   None go so far
As those who know not whither they are going.
    Iret.   Better go far than not to go at all !
But for this Cromwell, Sirs, you know he is
My leader and my friend : and much I love him :
And love unravels oft the bosom's page,
Where jealousy at fault misreads the whole.
So from my love I'll strive to paint him to you.
   Lamb.   So do, we'll hear you as an oracle.
    Iret.   Well, then, he is no common trivial man,
Who as a zany simply is a zany,
Can do one thing, no more.   The time has been
I've seen him in one day, 'twixt morn and even,
Preach, win a battle, bloodstained preach again, .
(Hugh Peters could not readier) : while his hearers,
With souls in heaven, already parted, drew
Grace from him as an angel.   Yet once more,
By camp-fire light, see him the revel's lord

Amid his troopers clink the flowing can,
And suit the merry story to the hour,
Their idol and their darling.   This till night,
Till time of council ! then once more behold him,
Ardent yet sage, bold and adroit by turns,
In speech not eloquent, yet i' the soul of speech,
Wisdom, a very Nestor !   Trust him, friends !
He says not much : waits long : but his quick deeds
Outstrip his words, and what he once has done
Needs no twice-doing : 'tis Jove's thunderbolt
That, where it falls, leaves ashes.   No such man
Earth saw till now, all wonders mixed in one,
Confusion, discords, all attuned in him,
Our Maccabean Cæsar.   Trust him then !
Were he but here——

> *Crom.* (*who has entered unawares.*)   Trust him, he'd
> buffet you !   (*Suiting the deed to the word.*)
>
> *Iret.*   What you here, General ?
>
> *Crom.*   Ha ! (*Fencing at him.*) You thought me dead,

And were in act to write my epitaph :
I have fared better in these Northern wars.

> *Iret.*   Welcome, whenever come ! thrice welcome now !

What from the army ?

> *Crom.*   Not a Scot in England

Twixt Dee and Tweed, not captive or a corpse !

> *Lud.*   Well done !
>
> *Har.*   Brave army !
>
> *Iret.*   Noble General !
>
> *Crom.*   Give God the glory, all the glory, Ireton !

Nothing to man !   We are but instruments :
The foe were but as stubble to our swords.

But of thy news ? Those men in Westminster, .
Those prating men ! I say the Parliament ?
How fare they with their ceaseless Aye and Nay,
Prating, not doing, with a tilt of words,
As if all life were but a tournament ?
If in the world I do mislike a man,
'Tis he who, set as pilot at the helm,
Lets swift occasion slip unheeded by,
And thinks and talks, and talks and thinks again,
Barren of aught but windy argument.

  Lud. Trouble no more about them !

  Crom.   How ! you dared ?

  Lud. We purged it.

  Crom.   Well ?

  Lud.   'Twill need no purging more.

  Crom. They are our own?

  Lud.   They are.

  Crom.   And of the King ? [*A pause.*
How mean you, Sirs ? No answer ! Hath the King——

  Hutch. We were discussing, Cromwell, of the King,
E'en as you entered.

  Crom.   Ha ! What said you of him ?

  Hutch. That he must die.

  Crom. .   Is't so ?

  Hutch. .   The man of blood
Be gathered to his victims.

  Crom.   So, indeed ?

  Hutch. By open trial solemnly condemned.

  Crom. Aye, truly ?

  Lud.   And thus knowing thine high office,
The love and favour that the army bear thee——

Crom. By trial ?

Lud. (*Angry.*) Say for what or whom art thou ?

Crom. Thine, if thou studiest the peace of England !
Else thy fixed foe !   Count ye the cost of this ?

Lud. In sooth but little.

Crom.   It will multiply
Your foes, already legion.

Lud.   We can meet them.

Crom. 'Twixt you and them set gulphs impassable.

Lud. No matter ! So we reign with Lazarus
In Abraham's breast, let Dives howl below !

'   *Crom.* And everything will then run . new   in
     England.

Hutch. Better it should, than patch old cloth with
     new !

Crom. The people love their ancient monarchs well.

Hutch. And their God little : time it were to cure
     them !

Crom. Aye true, you chide me well. We trust too
     much
In feeble crutches, things of carnal wisdom,
Weak instruments at best.   It was not these
Led us thus far, from worse than Egypt's bondage,
Poor humble men and few against the mighty,
Earth's terrible and great ones : no, not these.
'Twas a divinity that led us on,.
With signs in Heaven, and providences clear,
Dread dispensations of the Almighty's hand,
Dark to the host of Pharaoh, to our eyes
Far-shining, clear, unclouded.   [*A pause.*
                              Yet to slay him !

I grieve, I grieve, I could be grieved to death
To have to do it.
    Hutch.   And hast thou no grief
For others, for the Cause? '
    Crom.   It shall not perish.
It cannot, Sirs. Better a hundred kings,
Each scion of a hundred ancestors,
Should die ere it.
    Lud.   Then wherefore dost thou pause?
    Iret. What is the question?
    Crom.   Will this settle England?
As Christian men, and also men of honour,   :
That is the only question for us all.
If there be any here can settle England
At his feet I would kneel, and lay me down—
Aye that I would—in humblest reverence.
But for this plan, this one particular plan,
Truly I doubt. The King! I am not clear.
The Cause! It must not, no, it shall not die.
Would God but guide us! To shed innocent blood
Were murder, hateful, devilish. Yet the King
Is guilty: God hath shown it, and our swords,
Ha!   .   *[A noise without.*
Enter HUGH PETERS, *and soldiers wearing red scarfs:*
    they present a petition.
·   *Crom.* (*Taking it.*) Unto which of us is this?
    Hugh Peters. Unto thee, O General.
.   *Crom.* (*Reads.*) ' In the name of the most pious and·
godly army, unto whom mercies have been vouchsafed
of the Lord, many and glorious, with pouring out of
blood, and breaking of vials : we do ask, with all humility,

and reverence, for justice : justice on the chief delinquent, even on Charles Stuart; that as Agag was not
spared, when the Amalekites were smitten, so '——Ha !
Sirs, this squares with our conclusion. From whence
come you ?

1st Sold. Verily from the town called Windsor, after
a solemn exercise of prayer and general abasement.

Crom. And you would have justice upon Charles ?

1st Sold. Of a truth yes, most mighty General. Up,
and sanctify the people, even as Joshua the son of Nun
did in the valley of Achor, Joshua vii. 24 ; and cast out
the accursed thing from among us, lest we be smitten
before our enemies as at the first.

Crom. Ah, Sirs, this is a great matter, truly a great
matter that ye have in hand.

1st Sold. And one, we are minded, which brooks
no delay.

Crom. That shall be, as it shall be : no more, no less.

1st Sold. But, Sir, the army——

Crom. Sirrah, the army is nothing but what its
leaders will it. Go back, and wait the trumpet. Then
prepare you for the battle. We will see to this.

Hugh Peters. Stay, for the Spirit is upon me.
(*Hiding his face in his hands. A pause, then
withdrawing them.*)

It is revealed, it is revealed to me. Ye shall smite
him, ye shall smite the accursed, not secretly nor in
a corner, but before all Israel, and before the sun.
Wherefore do their kings ride in chariots, and their nobles
sit in purple and fine linen ? Verily their purple shall be
dabbled with blood, and their chariots broken in sunder.

as with a whirlwind. Is it not written of old, and the word remaineth? ' Bind their kings in chains, and their nobles in fetters of iron.' Therefore shall ye try him, where the great ones are tried, even at Westminster : and to the scaffold and the axe shall ye doom him : so by his blood shall England be redeemed, and tyrants shall tremble over all the world for ever.

1st Sold. It is the will of God : it is the will of God : we are not free to reject this voice.

Hugh Peters. And I have a message unto thee, O leader.[4] Like Moses, like Moses, thou art destined to take this people out of the bondage of Egypt. This army must root up monarchy not only here but in France, and in other kingdoms round about. This army is that corner-stone cut out of the mountain which must dash the powers of the earth in pieces. This is an age to make examples and precedents.   [*Soldiers show approval.*

Iret. (*To Cromwell who is hesitating*). Cromwell, indeed it is necessity.

Lud. He speaks the truth, we must kill or be killed. Weak counsels, and weak acting undo all.

Hutch. The army crumbles into mutinies. The Parliament will soon relift its head.

Lud. I will not answer for one single man, Scarce for myself, if this thing may not be.

Crom. What would ye have me?

Lud.   Lead us as of old, Reaping the rout, and driving victory home, And with the ridding of one plague, rid all !

Hugh Peters. See, see ! a door is open. Woe to us

                    ·⁴ See Appendix.

if we enter not in ! Prophecies are fulfilling round us.
Woe unto those whose heart is backward or indifferent !
If there be any such fainthearted, let them begone. Is it
not written, ' Cursed be he that doeth the work of the
Lord negligently !' 'Cursed be he whose sword is not
swift to shed blood !'

>   [*Agitation among the soldiers: shouts of ' The*
>   *sword of the Lord and of Gideon.' ' To*
>   *your tents, O Israel.'*]

Crom. (*striding into the midst.*) How, mutiny ! ye
        dare ! Have ye no grace
Among you ? So, fall back !

>   [*They retire in confusion to the back of the stage.*
>   Yet, they have reason ! [*Aside.*
There is a vein of something more than reason
In the crowd's noise : though, as the torrent's course,
It must be led to good : it must be led.

Lud. Yield !

Iret.   Nay, it is not yielding. Go right on,
Whither were tending all our steps before !

Lud. Be bold !

Iret.   For sake of England ! Shall she serve
A tyrant ?

Crom. Never !

Hutch.   Shall her gospel doors
New-opened be new-closed, and famished souls
Kept hungering, parted from the bread of heaven ?

Crom. Never again !

Hutch.   And shall blood-guiltiness
Be pardoned ? All the suffering, all the sin ?

Crom. Must it be so ? Is there no way of mercy ?

O Tyranny, oh, wert thou but a name !
Could we but slay thee without shedding blood,
Or bring thee, better, humbled to submission !
It may not be.   The baseness in the blood,   ·
(Ye know it, Sirs, ye know our naughty heart,)
Needs stronger, deeper purging, must with blood
Be voided thence, how hardly then washed clean !
So comes it, when the offence is fully ripe,
The inherited, the old ancestral sin,
In Pharaoh born, and to his offspring cleaving,   .
Falls on a head, guilty or innocent,
Even as predestined.

  Iret.   Then the blow shall fall ?

  Crom. So say ye all ?

  Voices.   All, all ! so help us God !

  Crom. Your lips avow it ?

  Voices.   And our hearts approve it.

  Crom. And with your hands——

  Voices.   We'll clench our work begun.

  Crom.· Then be it so ! Since Providence will have it,
Consult we not with wretched flesh and blood,
Or dull-eyed doubts, or miserable fears !
God's Spirit calls : we hearken : what is man,
That he should thwart Him?   God is everything,
The poor soul nothing.   Now He calls us, now,
By word, by deed, by issues not forecast,
Births not of earthly bearing or begetting,
Strange providences, great appearances,
Voices within, and stirs without our souls—
'Tis our high calling.   Can we turn from it ?

  Iret. How wilt thou act in this great crisis, Cromwell ?

Crom.   Leave all to me !

Iret. ·   'Tis safe.

Lud.   We live.

Hutch.   He dies.   [*Exeunt, all but Cromwell.*

Crom.   He dies !   Yes, so 'twas written ere the stars
Rolled on their orbits, or the fiery sun
Started to run his course.   It was foreordered,
And in the eternal Book 'twas written of me,
That I should be his doom : I a poor worm,
But for repeated mercy, thrice, thrice outcast,
Of grace, not merit, merest grace elected
To be the scourge of kings.   What then affrights me ?
His death ?   Nay, had he crossed me in the field,
In pomp and power majestic, on his head
Wearing the crown of all his ancestors,
Should I have spared him ?   'Tis not that, not that :
No, nor his name !   What's in that word, a King,
Fear-mutter'd breath, fool-echoed syllable,
That rising it should scare us like a ghost
From our fixed constancy ?   'Tis not his name.
What then ?   For there is something here within :
Something that trembles, and with innocent voice
Cries like a frightened child, 'All is not well.'
Not well !   In times like these what can be well ?
What can be well when brothers meet in arms,
And slaughter brothers ?   'Tis a fearful strife,
But we who in its torrent dare adventure,
With giant-strokes, seeking the bright Beyond,
Like drowning swimmers we must clutch the best,
And call it well.   We must put sternness on :
Seem what we are not : act, and grow by acting,

Schooled to performance of our cruel part,
Fierce as the time, rude as the need requires,
And carry the matter through, and hurry it on
To the bloody end: then pity: not before.   [*Exit.*

SCENE III.—HALL IN WINDSOR CASTLE.

KING CHARLES *and Servants.*

K. Charles.   What is't o'clock?

Serv.   'Tis nigh the hour of dinner:
Where will your Majesty be served to-day?

K. Charles.   Here, in the hall of state, immediately!
And hark thee, bid our chamberlains attend,
And spread above our royal canopy.   [*Exit Servant.*
How many monarchs here have sat in state!
How many courtiers waited on the knee!
And tired of dalliance, sick of droning peace,
For battles longed, longed to put armour on,
Bestride their chargers, hurry to the field,
And burn though but an hour, in glorious war,
Not smoulder on unused in idleness!
Ah, me! could we but change.   They wear my crown,
My crown of thorns!   I take their quiet graves,
Their deep, deep dreamless sleep, their obscure graves,
And rest, nor evermore hear faction's howl
Bay o'er my head, or muttering hatred turn
The milk of loyal bosoms into gall!
Then strife rage on, disorder hold thy sway!
Reason, sound doctrine, reverence, good will,
These are the melodies that make life sweet:

F

Without them all is mere discordancy.
And these being dead, gone, vanished from the world,
Why should I love to linger? Ha, who comes?

Enter HERBERT, *who presents letters: after him gentlemen
of the royal household, with servants, &c.*

Her. Letters, my liege!
K. Charles. Good Herbert, give me them.
How came they?
Her. By a worthy gentleman,
Disguised, from Ireland.
K. Charles. Ormond's hand and seal!
Now blessing light on that true nobleman!
What, hither, Herbert! Guess what I have heard?
Her. Good news, my liege, 'tis written in thy face.
K. Charles. Well may it! Hope, even in my
    hopelessness,
Like the Aurora in a Polar night,
Revives to cheer me. Come to dinner now,
Thou shalt beside me stand, and there hear all.
            [*The King dines, sitting in state, under a
            canopy: lords, chamberlains, and servants of
            his household in attendance.*
Ireland is faithful, Ormond writes me word,
Bursting to flames, and my dear Queen (Heaven keep
    her!
A woeful husband to her have I been)
Rouses the fair French lilies to our aid.
Denmark too wavers. Thus three cards are left,
Three playing chances in the game of war,

The worst of which played by a skilful hand
May win back everything.   But thou art silent.

    Her.   Ah, Sire !

    K. Charles. . What, doubt ?   The three things needed
       most :

Ships, men, and money! Denmark, Ireland, France !
The stubborn North, the fiery-hearted South,
And all already on their way to aid us !
O friend, you have lived too long in prison walls ;
You should go forth, and breathe sweet country air,
Hear the lark sing, and smell the blossomed rose ;
So bring the colour back into the cheek
Of pallid fear, and sad despondency.

    Her. (*Kneels*)   Pardon, my Master !

    K. Charles.   Rise, I did not chide thee.

    Her.   Ah, Sire, too flattering hope has been thy foe.

    K. Charles.   Hope ! 'tis my food, my clothing, 'tis
       my all :

My life's sole sustenance.   Who takes hope from me,
Strips from the beggar his one lingering rag,
Last shelter from the pelting pitiless storm :
And drives the outcast from the sanctuary
Forth to the wild again.   Give kinder counsel !

    Her.   Which is more kind, to bid the shattered bark
Keep haven ; or advise it brave the storm ?

    K. Charles.   Yet Herbert see, the storm's worst power
       is over :

The sun is breaking out : we near the shore.

    Her.   The storm is past, the shore is waiting nigh ;
But look what armed breakers roll between.
The sunshine breaks : 'tis a deceitful glare.

K. Charles.   Enough ! I'll follow Hope, who follows
  me :

' Dum spiro spero.'   'Twas my motto, Herbert,
In brighter days, and I'll not yield it now.

    Enter COL. WYCHCOTT.

Col.   Begone !   What do ye here ?   Begone, I say !
   (*To the King's attendants.*)

Here, soldiers, drive me these time-servers hence.
Upon your peril !

 K. Charles.   Ha ! What churl is this?
What brutish-natured and ill-manner'd churl
Gives orders here ?

 Her.   It is the Governor.

 K. Charles.   Sir, by what power enforce you this
  command ?

 Col.   The army's.

 K. Charles.   Worst of masters, sorriest slaves
Who do its bidding !   Yet upon what cause
Put you this insult on me?

 Col.   To prepare
For that shall follow after.

 K. Charles.   Sir, what mean you?
Wherefore this mystery ?

 Col.   King Herod trembles.

 Her.   This is too shameless.   Know you, Sir, to whom
And what you speak?

 Col.   You courtiers' days are over.

 K. Charles.   Suffer him, Herbert ! Rudeness is in
  favour ;

And sooner than be left behind the fashion,

He claps its most outrageous colour on,
And flares beyond it.   Time will teach him art :
'Till then, the piece is somewhat farcical.

    Col.   I am no flatterer.

    K. Charles.   'Tis above you, friend :
Ere you can flatter, you must rise to learn
The very alphabet of courtesy.

    Col.   Kings must hear truth.

    K. Charles.   True, and the truth is precious :
'Tis lovely, serviceable, rare, and brilliant :
'Tis the chief jewel in the crown of kings :
But truth needs gentle setting.   Its rude shape
Is hideous, uglier than a common stone.
And better falsehood in the true of heart,
Than truth itself on lips of falsity !

    Col.   Yet one thing more !   Your servants all must
      leave you.

    K. Charles.   My servants leave me, all ?   What, not
      one left ?
Stripped bare as Lear !

    Col.   I'll find you chamberlains
More honest if less mannered.   Corporal,
Be thou the King's obedient cupbearer !
And thou——

    K. Charles.   It needs not, Sir, this contumely :
You have the power, yet use it gently.   God,
Who made you man, made you for noble ends,
To lighten, not to load, the back of sorrow,
Crushing the fallen !   Now farewell outer pomp,
Henceforth I'll study to be great within :
For crimson mantle, vain imperial gaud,

I'll wear Christ's robe, long-suffering gentleness :
For spotless ermine put pure patience on :
And then—for earthly power is as a wheel,
What now is low, a turn may elevate—
I'll sit, and meeting mockery with a smile,
Tarry God's leisure, till at last men come
To know my innocent heart, my aim to serve
My office, not myself. Oh this is noble,
This is the martyr's way of overcoming,
This is true Christian ! Better than doubtful arms,
Than bloodshed, than battalions in the field ;
Better than war, hate-born and breeding hate !
This heavenly resignation. Come, good Herbert,
Let us away ! forget my hopes, my plottings ;
Patience be all my hope, my plotting now !

     [*His servants kneel about him, weeping.*

 K. Charles. Alas, true hearts ! I may not keep you.
    See ! (*To the Governor.*)
You can command their absence, not their tears,
That flow unbid in loving contumacy.
Yet cease your weeping ! Set in the power of man
It lies to cudgel us, to the worst of deeds
Adding worse words : but, friends, to suffer from them,
Quiver beneath that lash, avow that pain,
Lies not in others' violence, but ourselves,
In our too weak endurance. Go, farewell !

      [*They prepare to depart.*

 Col. Yet by your leave——
 K. Charles.   What more ?
 Col.   The army orders——
 K. Charles. Say forces, rather.

Col.   You leave Windsor, and
Depart for London.
  K. Charles.   God is everywhere,
Alike in wisdom, mighty power, and goodness.
To Him I trust.   Do what ye will with me !
This terrible fierce course must have an end.   ·
    [*Soldiers gather round the King, and his attendants ;
        then, rushing forward—*
Her.   Ye shall not take him.
K. Charles.   Peace ! 'tis theirs to order
Who now are masters.   In rebellion, swords
Grow into sceptres, sceptres shrink to straws.
                        [*Exeunt, guarded by soldiers.*

ACT IV.

SCENE I.—ROOM IN A HOUSE IN LONDON.

FAIRFAX [5] *and* LADY FAIRFAX.

Lady F. O bloody treason! black and hideous
   crime !

Fair. How now, what news?

Lady F.   The farce of trial over,
The plot is drawing to its tragic close.

Fair. Speak plainer, wife. This is no Christmas
   morn
To deal in riddles.

Lady F.   No, it is the eve
Of more than Lenten sorrows. It is rumoured
(Hark, how the soldiers clamour in the streets,
Like hounds full-cry, the royal hart in view !)
The King is to be sentenced. Speak, is it false,
Or is it true?

Fair.   It is, alas ! too true.

Lady F. Alas, that I should hear you say, Alas !
Alas, that you should live to say, Alas !
And be my husband, more, alas, than all !

Fair. Blame others, wife ! your arrows touch not me.

---

[5] See Appendix.

Lady Fair. Not you, my lord ? I thought you were
  the man,
Foremost and paramount in all this realm,
On whom it lies to curb these mettled spirits,
Which, checked, go easy as an ambling jade,
And dangerous only when not bridled in.
If I am wrong——
  Fair.   No more, I will not have it.
This is a civil business, and doth touch
The civil powers, not those who wear the sword.
  Lady F.   Ah, yes, I know you wash your hands of it :
You have no obligation.   Pilate sits,
And with his legions armed enforces peace,
While Innocence hangs bleeding.   Noble Pilate !
It was a priestly business, and did touch
The priestly powers, not him who wore the sword.
  Fair.   I do not wish his death.
  Lady F.   No more did Pilate.
  Fair.   I fain would save him.
  Lady F.   So would Pilate also.
  Fair.   But how to do it ?   Advise me : woman's wit,
In fault of reason, reason to itself,
Oft outruns man, as doth the early thorn
Bloom, while the slow oak lingers.
  Lady F.   How, my lord, ·
You ask me how ?   If you, supreme in all,
Wish not his death, and say it shall not be,
Why then in all this little world of England,
From Southern Foreland up to John o' Groats,
What man so bold to dare to force it on ?
  Fair.   Cromwell !

Lady F.   Still Cromwell?   Nothing but that name?
There surely was a certain Fairfax once
On whom this Cromwell waited, cap in hand,
To take instruction from his general.
Is all this alter'd?   What?   Is Fairfax nothing?
(For second after first is last of all,)
While Cromwell is a name to rouse the dead,
A spell of power, a majesty of sound,
That fills all England to the farthest seas.

    Fair.   Tush, wife!

    Lady F.   Your name is to a byword grown.
'Tis said (my love incites me to re-echo
What others say in scorn), 'tis said, 'smooth Jacob
Has overreached plain Esau.'

    Fair.   Ha! they say it.

    Lady F.   But pardon, I have vexed you.

    Fair.   Nay, no fear!

    Lady F.   What matter, so our conscience sting us not,
For all the babble rumour in the streets?

    Fair.   The public jest!

    Lady F.   Nay, Cromwell is not Jacob.

    Fair.   Duped, and by him!

    Lady F.   Is it, alas! too true?

    Fair.   Peace, wife, your words bring madness.   Close,
       dark man!
His arts have led me to the precipice,
Where is no standing, whence is no return.

    Lady F.   How do you mean, my lord?

    Fair.   Pretending zeal,
Like Gideon, to have none but godly men,
He purged the army of its loyal stuff

To fill it with his creatures.   Fool, thrice fool !
                                        [*Beating his head.*
  Lady F. And is all lost?
  Fair.   All, yes, I fear me all.
For I was but a soldier, and I sought
A soldier's end—to conquer : and for that
Still craved more soldiers.   So the blade would cut,
I cared not whose the name upon the steel,
Fairfax or Cromwell.   But not so this man,
Looking far on : contriving distant ends
(O damnedest cunning to appear most simple !)
Through tortuous means, he would have none with him
Not wholly his, body and soul and all,
Pledged to his eyebrows' prompting.   Therefore now,
Following his lead, scheming with him together,
The camp is whirling like a parliament,
Each with his cry, For God ! for his arrears !
For vengeance on the great delinquent, Charles !
None for his duty merely : none to obey
His general's word.
  Lady F. And you?
  Fair.   I humoured them.
  Lady F. Alas, alas, I have been so proud of you,
My husband.
  Fair. 'Sdeath!   It is the time's worst plague ;
None can be trusted.   Honest and true men
Are tricked of villains : brothers undo brothers :
Nay, very words of noblest ancestry,
From honour parted, sink to vilest meaning ;
Till wisdom is a name for serpent's wile,
And simpleness the fool's simplicity.

Alas ! and so it comes in such a time
That the best cause, served by the best of men,
Give but a turn to shifty Fortune's wheel,
Turns out the worst.   Oh to have seen this once,
When not too late, or to be blind for ever !
                              [*A bell is heard tolling.*
    Lady F.   Hark ! 'tis the call to action !   Ere that bell
Have ceased its knelling, it may be too late,
Too late for aught but penitence.   O husband,
Think that a life is set upon the cast
More dear to each in England than his own,
Than sister, son, or sire, than wife, than all :
And that of England's myriads one alone,
One only can preserve him !   That man, thou !
Here, take thy sword !   A blot is on its blade :
Thy helm !   A stain is on its knightly plume.
Go, furbish them in honour's fountain clean,
As is the snowy blossom on a maid,
For her chaste bridal newly garlanded !
Quick ! 'tis the living moment is our own :
To-morrow's chance is given to other hands :
Furies pursue the man of sloth for ever.
Quick ! what thou doest must be done now—to-day !
To-day ! and ere night's angel seal up all
To condemnation, Time with Time's misdeeds,
Come back triumphant, crowned with double fame :
As once rebuker of a tyrant's pride,
His saviour now from hate's worse tyranny.
    Fair.   I go : if not too late, I'll save the king,
Or else——
    Lady F.   What else ?

Fair.   My office abdicating
I will depart, and in some far off land
Hide my shamed head, and pray good Englishmen
To pardon all the ills my fault brings on them,
And not too much to curse me being gone.   [*Exit.*.
   Lady F. Go! and shall I, forsooth, as weak of arm,
Shall I, because a woman, stay behind,
And bear no part in this great controversy?
Nay, grief, like madness, doth unsex us all!
And women of a clay exceeding gentle
In heat of suffering grow, as marble, hard:
While men of iron, robuster, battle-hardened,
Shrink, in the trial melting.   I will go,
Will seek yon hall, and there in treason's face,
'Fore all men, too ashamed to think of shame,
My voice—oh, had it but a trumpet's blazon!
A woman's voice, when chivalry is dumb,
Shall break the silence, and in traitors' hearing
Cry vengeance, vengeance for a murdered King!

SCENE II.—ROOM IN CROMWELL'S HOUSE.

CROMWELL, *and* JOHN CROMWELL *his cousin.*[6]

Crom. Welcome, good cousin, both to me and England!

John C. To you and England! Why not England first?
Who made her second to your Majesty?

* See Appendix.

Crom. Tush, to your business !   Things, not words,
   to-day !

John C. God grant the word betoken not the thing :
But to my task ! ˊ This signet which I bear
Commissions me the States' Ambassador !

Crom. Good ; and your end ?

John C.   To save you from a deed
Whose matchless horror shall make Europe arm,
Led by her kings, ten thousand thousand men,
To come and wash this stain clean from the earth,
Like an unnatural birth of bestial sin ;
And drown the accursed island in the seas,
Out of the sight of shuddering Christendom.

   Crom. Peace with your threats !   We are not aspen
   leaves,
To waver for a breath of angry wind.

   John C.   Yet, cousin, by the common blood we bear,
Our mutual love ; by our two fathers' bones
Entombed together in one sepulchre,
Turn from this deed, this damned hideous deed,
Which, let as many years roll o'er thy grave
As since the death of Him on Calvary,
Will still live on fresh in the minds of men,
Will never let our name rest from reproach,
But hunt it still with whips of ignominy :
Till our descendants, weary and ashamed,
Shunned at the mart, banned from the courteous feast,
Passed with averted horror in the streets,
Shall curse the fate that linked their lot with thine,
And study to be called by any name,
But that of their ill-famous ancestor.

Crom. So let it be! Let hatred dog my life!
Malice rake up my ashes after death!
So I free England, so that o'er my grave
Those lips be free that curse my memory.

   John C. What seek you?

   Crom.   Freedom!

   John C.   That has been in England
Since time of Alfred.

   Crom.   That has never been
Till now. Seven years ago, (remark this well:
If a man scruple at the plain clear truth
'Tis vain to argue with him,) in this land,
This Christian land, reformed since Henry's time,
It was a shame to call oneself a Christian.

   John C. Why make you not agreement with the
      King?

   Crom. With him? What, any good from that false
      man,
Against whom Heaven has witnessed? Good from him?

   John C. You say, he's false.

   Crom.   And if I said it not,
These very walls would say it. Nay, the things,
I say, the things have voices in themselves.

   John C. But——

   Crom.   Yes, for all his features look so fair,
Cursed with the grace weak fools and women love,
So grand, so calm, so like a gentleman,
Yet that fair mask hides ugly-shapen thoughts,
Which in poor men were called by ugly names;
In short, you know him not to plead his cause.

   John C. Yet, kinsman, once I heard you pity him,

And say he was a harmless injured man,
And swear to right him, even with the sword.

    Crom. I did.

    John C.   And now?

    Crom.   I am a dupe no more.

I tell you, John, I have seen it; seen the proof,
In his own hand, of his great perfidy.

    John C. Yet kill him? Slay a man for things like
       these,

Granting them true?'

    Crom.   It is necessity :

'Tis he or we. If he remount his throne,
Then all that we have purchased with our blood——

    John C. What's that?

    Crom. What's that? The one thing in the world
Makes life worth living, Gospel liberty !
Assure me that. and I will sheathe my sword
Even in his bosom who opposes peace :
If not, beware the man who crosses me !

    John C. And is there nought but this?

    Crom.   Would Heaven there were !

Believe me, I am not a bloody man.
I have shed tears when men like shatter'd logs
Strewed the red earth, and groanings filled the air :
And victory's eve was sadder than the morn
That marshalled me perchance to infamy.
But for the Cause, (mark me !) the Cause I love,
(Truly, who would not die for such a Cause ?)
I would as lief shoot down my father's son,
Albeit he stood in likeness of my mother,
And sued for mercy as the midnight wolf,

Whose stealthy prowl marks him for murderer.

John C. O iron man !

Crom.   The iron is in him

Who goads me to it.

John C.   You'll not spare him then ?

Crom. No more than he would me !

John C.   Then, ere I go,

        (*Locks the door: draws something from his breast.*)

To use my sole remaining argument.

Crom. (*Drawing a pistol from his bosom.*) What,
        from a kinsman ?

John C.   Put your weapon up,

And cease your fears : I am no murderer.

(*Showing a paper to Cromwell who reads and returns it.*)

        Crom. Unlock that door, and put your offer up :

And know that baubles cannot tempt a man

Whose heart is set above this earthly sphere.

Speak not to me ! 'tis Heaven has fixed this doom :

And how shall I, who hope to merit Heaven,

Like Judas, for a paltry price of money,

Sell my dear soul to hinder its decrees ?

        John C. Yet honour, riches, titles, weigh them well.

        Crom. Yes, honour, riches, titles, there are men

Who would accept them, and invent fair names

To gloze the foul deed to their consciences.

        John C. Look upon England's proudest families !

Their founders won those titles by the sword.

        Crom. As I might do, and they are honoured now,

And long will be : and 'tis an honoured thing

To rank as one of England's noblemen.

        John C. He yields. (*Aside.*)

                        G

Crom.   Who are the sureties to the bond?

John C. The Prince of Orange and the Prince of Wales.

Crom. Both noted names, and worthy gentlemen.

John C. And you shall be in all things next the King.

Crom. A place of honour for a man to hold!

John C. And guide his conscience as his Minister.

Crom. Indeed an office to be coveted!

John C. And freedom have to worship as you will.

Crom. A righteous and a necessary thing!

John C. And fill the land with your conventicles.

Crom. Tempter, begone! I did but tamper with you,
To sound your baseness.   Put your offer up!
Unlock that door and let the whole world in,
To see a man who scorns such infamy.

JOHN CROMWELL *opens the door, and enter* MRS. CROMWELL.

Mrs. C. Why this loud voice? this outburst, Oliver?
Cousin, you here?

Crom.   Oh yes, be kind to him!
For, as I live, indeed he loves me well.

Mrs. C. What seeks he here?

Crom.   The safety of the King.

Mrs. C. My aim as well.

Crom.   You too?

Mrs. C.   I cannot rest,
Or rise, and gaze upon the wintry stars,
But spectre-like, betwixt me and the night,
Paler, more ghastly than the freezing moon,
Looms his sad face, banishing sleep.   It moves not,
Speaks not, says nothing in reproach : but silent,

Silent as death, and pale as alabaster,
Death's image on an ice-cold marble tomb, -
It follows me, and mute with pleading eyes,
Upbraids me more than words. O Cromwell, Crom-
. well!

Crom. What would you, woman?

Mrs. C.　　　　　　,Spare him, husband, spare him.

Crom. He is not sentenced.

Mrs. C.　　　　　　No, but he is doomed,
I know it, certain as to-morrow, doomed :
And you have doomed him. Let me read your face.
Do not I dearly know each line of mercy
In those loved features? and where are they now?

Crom. Tush, wife, begone!

Mrs. C.　　　　　　'. O spare him, you have power;
You sentence, and you pardon.

Crom.　　　　　　He is guilty.

Mrs. C. So are we all, all guilty ; and the offender
Must suffer, even the loftiest: yet, bethink you,
Has he not suffered?

Crom. '　　　And has nothing learnt
By all his suffering.

Mrs. C.　　　Liberty's a piece
That must be oft rehearsed, ere it go well.
From king to clown, all have their separate parts,
And one offending part may spoil the whole ;
Yet oft, 'tis seen, rehearsals, raw at first,
Prelude the best of action.

Crom. .　　　Peace, he dies.

Mrs. C. And at your hand?

Crom.　　　Nay! God, not I, hath judged him.

Mrs. C.   Some make a god of their own cruel hearts.

Crom.   Some will not hearken when the Spirit calls.

Mrs. C.   Some speak of justice when they mean
    revenge.

Crom.   Some dare not, out of weakness, to be just.

Mrs. C.   And dare you shed the life-blood of a king?

Crom.   As well as he the blood of other men.

Mrs. C.   You will not spare him?

Crom.   Not though all on earth,
Not though an angel out of Heaven, plead for him!

Enter MRS. CLAYPOLE.[7]

Mrs. C.   Nay, let one plead on earth. Come hither,
    daughter!

Mrs. Clay.   Is it too late?

Mrs. C.   Entreat him!

Mrs. Clay.   O my father,
Be pitiful!

Crom.   To whom? To you, and all
That's best in England?

Mrs. Clay.   Nay, they need no pity.

Crom.   Pity the wolf, who captive weeps false tears
But have no pity on the slaughtered lambs
Who cannot weep?

Mrs. Clay.   I have no skill in words:
No art of fence, or tricks of argument;
Those use, who plead in an unrighteous cause!
Yet, father, for the sake of all you love,
For honour, virtue, love of peace, good name,
Your good, and all men's, soil not victory's close,

.[7] See Appendix.

The blessedest victory ever crowned men's arms,
With foulness of revenge.
 Crom.   He's full of danger
To those you love.
 Mrs. Clay.   Less in his life than death !
Living, his errors disinherit him :
Dead, his slain virtues will as incense rise,
And blind beholders to his tyranny.
 Crom. I cannot spare him.
 Mrs. Clay.   Cannot ? You the shield,
The sword of England ?
 Crom.   Cannot spare a man
Whom God has sentenced.
 Mrs. Clay.   God in many voices
Speaks to men's hearts, not only thundertongued,
Nor in the earthquake dealing doom ! but after,
In still-toned whispering mercy. Hear it, father,
Hear it, your heart inclines you. Let him live
Like a caged eagle, weak, with broken wing,
T' attest the skill and power of that true arm
Which marked the robber sailing near the sun,
And struck him low—then spared him. Oh you weep,
You still have tears.
 Crom.   I weep, but not for him.
 Mrs. Clay. Yet weep ! One tenderness may breed
  another :
Green islands in the snow till all is green.
 Crom. What will you ?
 Mrs. Clay. Life is such a sacred thing !
Is there no way to purify the shrine,
But battering the holiest temple down ?

No way to make him humble? none to bend
His high proud spirit?   Oh tell me, thou so kind,
Who wouldst not tread the path for the crushed worm,
Nor turn a beggar from thy door away,
Must his blood flow? his blood, whose unwashed stain,
Rustlike corroding where it fouls for ever,
Lives on the hand that shed it, yet no more
Comes back to warm its natural cheek again?
O father!

 Crom. Ask me something for thyself:
All shall be thine.

 Mrs. Clay. What I do ask for him
Is for myself.   Nay rather (woman's heart,
Rich but in loving, knows no private gain)
'Tis for thee also, father.

  Crom.   Aught but this!

 Mrs. Clay. Aught!   Oh, as thou hast lived in blaze
  of honour,
Matchless, unrivalled, in these glorious wars,
Let no dark cloud across the brightness come!
Let not men say, Thus far, so much was well:
Then came a change, an after-twilight hour
Eclipsing all: then grew the glory dim.

 Crom. My child!

 Mrs. Clay.   Be this thy children's heritage,
To boast, He had a nation in his hand,
A monarch, prize of conquest, at his feet,
And he showed mercy.

   (*A pause:* CROMWELL *much shaken: then a trumpet*
    is heard—he starts.)

 Crom. Hark! I dally here,

When duty calls me as a clarion. Hence !
Man that is born of woman still has much
Of woman in him : still the lower Eve
Beguiles the loftier Adam of our souls,
And makes men forfeit Eden. Rise, my heart ;
Rise, better friend, and mounting tread down weakness !
The devil through our virtues else doth tempt us,
When we our sins have master'd. I'll no more.
The cruelest justice is the kindest mercy.
He never pitied. Hence ! The man must die.

Enter FAIRFAX.

Fair. Cromwell, you have deceived me.
Crom. Ha ! another ?
Cousin, wife, daughter, he who should be most
With me, against me ! Come ! my heart is proof—
Come all at once ! I can sustain you all.
Fair. The troops are drawing through the streets.
The trial
Commences straight. The public expectation
Forebodes a sentence.
Crom. They forebode aright.
Fair. Was this your promise ?
Crom. What ?
Fair. To study peace
And for this end to live, to die——
Crom. For England !
Fair. What means that sudden name ?
Crom. To some men all !
To others—God awake their sleeping souls !—
Less even than nothing !

Fair.   Sirrah, I love England.

Crom.   Then come with me at once to Westminster.

Fair.   Violent man ! I hate these bloody ways.

Crom.   Pitiful man, to stop so near a goal !

Fair.   Blood ! what more blood ? will nought but
    blood content you ?

Must we with sacrifices glut our land,

Make Golgothas of every smiling plain,

And slay on scaffolds those who scaped the sword,

Till none are left but ghosts ? Yet stay, I bid you—

One effort more—on your allegiance, Cromwell !

    Crom.   I own a greater Master in my soul.

    Fair.   Your General bids you.

    Crom.   If he bid me arm

Against my Cause, my country, and my God,

Away ! he is no General of mine.

    Fair.   I'll rouse the army.

    Crom.   They are for his death.

    Fair.   For they're your creatures, and I'm nothing
      now

Where still in name I'm all. O Cromwell, Cromwell,

Surely it had been nobler in the field,

To have assailed me, struck me, beat me down,

Leave me a record of thy rage and valour,

Than unsuspecting thus, and from behind,

To stab me in mine honour. Nay, but hear me :

I will be heard. Think not that I am made

So slavishly, of such weak yielding stuff,

As with a soul abhorrent to thy deeds,

Mutely to work thy will. Here, take my sword !

'Tis yours by conquest. Take it ; 'tis a blade

Has seen much service, won no little honour,
In Freedom's cause. But, now it is degraded,
Enslaved, made instrument of vilest using,
I scorn to wear it longer.
    Crom. ·   Why, what's this?
Are you mad, General? Is all the world
Brainsick and doting on a worthless King,
Gone mad and blind at once? Take back your sword !
Take it, and now in calmness answer me.
Trust you the King?
    Fair.   I do not.
    Crom.   Truly said !
Were he again upon his father's throne,
What would you do?
    Fair.   Withdraw to my estate——
    Crom. And study safety. Truly said again.
How then would fare your holy Covenant?
    Fair. I fear but badly.
    Crom.   And the men who shed
Their blood like water in this sacred cause?
    Fair. Indeed I know not.
    Crom.   But I know right well.
The dreariest den, the oldest-rusted chain,
The wretchedest pallet, and the mouldiest fare,
This, Fairfax, were those heroes' courtly thanks
Whose swords saved England. Nay, you wrong yourself
To plead his cause : in truth you wrong us all.
If he do live, 'tis but a man the more,
Another thorn in a waste wilderness :
Fresh evil, where there is too much already :
While if he die, a thousand freedoms flourish

From out his grave, blessing a thousand lands,
To blossom on till time shall be no more.

    Fair. Well, go your way ! I wash my hands of it.

    Crom. At your good pleasure. Come who will
      with me !

In sooth I care not. If it be a friend,
I ask him come : but if he scruple at me,
If he deny that faith by which I live,
I'll sweep him like a thistle from my path.

    Mrs. C. Yet stay !

    Crom.   . I'll do it in despite of all ;
Aye, though it be a tyranny to do it,
Nevertheless I glory in the deed.

    Mrs. Clay. Be merciful !

    Crom.   Go to your chamber, girl !
There never was a deed of duty done,
For the world's weal involving one man's woe,
But some fond woman wished. it otherwise.

    John C. And I !

    Crom.   I had forgot you, fare you well. .

    (*Offers his hand, which the other refuses.*)

'Tis well—begone ! This to your masters take
For our reply. If Europe come to England
With open hand, and unknit, smiling brow,
She shall have welcome : hospitable doors,
Whose bolts were forged to keep the stranger out,
Shall ope their widest to let strangers in :
And none shall then be foreign to our love,
But he who out of tune with this new time,
When Christian hearts 'gin chime to one accord,
Harps on the old string, ' Hate the foreigner.'

Thus much in friendship !   But if ill-advised,
Or envious, grudging freedom, malice-swollen,
They seek to tear one grain, one grain of dust,
From yon white cliffs, our virgin citadels,
Then though ten more Armadas hither come,
Europe and all her kings on board of them,
We fear them hot.   What England's head shall order,   :
That shall her hand make good against the world. [*Exit.*

    John C.   He kill the King ?   He kill the King ?   I
    fear   ·
'Twill not be long ere a new King appear.

                            [*Exeunt omnes.*

SCENE III.—ROOM IN ST. JAMES'S PALACE.

KING CHARLES *and* HERBERT.

    K. Charles.   The world is but a gaol.   We all are
    captives.
At best we know a little passing freedom
Betwixt our birth and graves.   E'en o'er our cradles   ɔ
The serpents gather.   Then in nurse's arms
To win admirers Cleopatra burns,   ·
While Cæsar grasps the moon with young ambition,   ˋ
And both begin their course.   Chained to their task
They toil, no bondslave harder : night and day   ˌɔ
The passion goads them on : yet, as their chain   .
Is gold and glittering, worn with idle noise, ˋ ·
Poor men oft envy them.   Yet trust me, Herbert,
A poor man knows more happiness than a king, .
Is freer, kindlier, lighter.   O the trifles,   ⁖ˋ
The tedious trifles graced with sounding names. ·

That eat a great man's time up !   Who would live
Sitting on thorns, subjected to the weight
Of envious eyes, fearing in all his realm
No breath but flattery's? sleep to dream of troubles ;
Then wake to find his nightlong vision true,
New foes, and old foes fiercer?   Who would be
Servant of all, slave of his veriest slave,
Climbing to Heaven, yet crushed down by the weight
Of a whole kingdom? but that to it born
We cannot cast the burden from our back ;
'Tis fixed, 'tis native to us : and He who made it,
He who made all things, once in shape of flesh
Himself endured the heaviest load of all,
Load of earth's sin, sin of the world that slew Him,
Leaving behind a pattern of true pain,
To shame the sigh of plaintive royalty.

> *Her.*   Speak on ! speak ever thus ! and let me
> listen

Words that shall after be my comforters :
Oh I am glad to see you, Sire, so tranquil !

> *K. Charles.*   Why should I not?   My struggles now
> are over.

The drowning swimmer suffers twenty deaths
Before he yields : that done, he sinks to sleep
Calm as on beds of roses.

> *Her.*   Yet they live

The cause of this.

> *K. Charles.*   So be it.
> *Her.*   They have wronged you.
> *K. Charles.*   Then let them live to feel their punish-
> ment !

Her.   But you—why should you suffer ?

K. Charles.   O my friend,
Humiliations bring us to the Cross,
And the Cross lifts us to the gates of Heaven :
And so uplifted, though on cruel wrong,
Who would arraign the wronger's cruelty?

Her.   Yet doth it grieve me, Sire, to hear them
       boast
God's sentence on you.

K. Charles.   Nay, if from success
They infer justice, then Iscariot's cause
Was holier than his Master's ; then the Martyr,
Whose last appealing glance is turned to Heaven,
Needs the forgiveness which his dying lips
Bequeath to his tormentors.   Nay, if Might,
Their creed, be Right, then must ye mint anew
The forgeries of language, coined to wear
The stamp of Justice, unmake every law,
Change every heart.   Why doth the solemn judge
Sit on the bench, the felon stand i' the dock ?
Reverse them !   Let the murderer try his strength
With the accuser !   Nay, what longer need
Of laws at all?   Each man's a law.   The giant
Law to the world, a Moses, Solomon,
Grand legislator for all time !   Let's follow
With blind mole-eyes harsh nature's cruel course,
Rend, tear, waste, ravin, as wild wolves prey on lambs,
Seek our weak opposites, and open-mouthed
Unmuzzled flesh our bloody reeking fangs !
Worship brute strength !   Why do we doting kneel
To dreams ?   The fool was right.   There is no God.

Her.　Thus grows the evil fruit of heresy,
Ripen'd at last: when every ranting rogue,
Cobler, mechanic, mouthing man of arms,
Prates as inspired, and adds for his own use,
A codicil to both the Testaments,
Commending murder and revenge.　O piteous!
Ruin of Nature, second fall of man!
O horrible, crying, and contagious sin,
Soon to infect all lands!　Now, from this time,
The little good that ever was on earth,
Still bright, sad record what the height we fell,
Perishes visibly ; and, order lost,
Rude chaos comes again.
　　K. Charles.　　　　　'Tis so, dear friend.
Yet worse remains behind.　O England, England,
Whose sons, sea-guarded from their foes without,
Eat up each other like fierce dogs within:
Torn by domestic strife, unhappy realm!
While thou didst love religion and thy king,
Wert thou not honoured? wert thou not esteemed?
For glory, beauty, riches, was there one
Of all earth's proudest empires mate for thee?
Then what nobility could match with thine?
What merchants with thy merchants?　Learning came
And, fixed in thee her lonely separate seat,
Her purer bowers, her lovelier Academe,
Taught wisdom new and old : and solemn awe,
Grace handed down from Apostolic hands,
Light not of earth, pure ray angelical,
Invested all thy priesthood.　Now, poor land,
Cast like the Prodigal to husks, and swine,

Degraded, name of infamy in the world,
How art thou changed, how fallen! Scan but thyself!
In the astonishment and scorn of men
Read thy dishonour! Thine own favourites crowned
Oppress thee more than in the worst of times
The worst of tyrants: and the traitorous sword—
Sword thou didst whet against thy lawful king—
Now pierces thine own bosom. I'll away,
And in my oratory pray awhile. [*Exit.*

Enter Colonels with armed men.

Col. 1. Who will announce it to him?
Col. 2. You. Not I.
Col. 2. Then you!
Col. 3. I, never! I would rather face
Bold Rupert and his fiery cavaliers,
With broken ranks, than come before him thus
With such a message.
Col. 1. See, himself he comes.

Enter KING CHARLES *from his oratory.*

K. Charles. What seek ye? Are ye dumb, or tongue-
less men?
Col. 1. It is the day.
K. Charles. Proceed.
Col. 2. The army orders——
K. Charles. Ominous name!
Col. 3. No more! I'll break it to him.
It is decreed you must go hence with us
To hear your sentence.
K. Charles. Ha! so soon?

Col. 3.   'Tis ordered.

K. Charles. By whom?

Col. 3.   By those who sent us.

K. Charles.   May I see
Your warrant?

Col. 3.   Here! (*pointing to his sword.*)

K. Charles.   Legibly writ indeed!
Where learnt you, sir, these most fair characters?

Col. 2. Blood must be shed for blood.

K. Charles.   Then make yourselves
The foremost victims! Not on me alone
Wreak all your rage!

Col. 2.   It is necessity.

K. Charles. Necessity! O God, how men presume
To usurp thine attributes! The highest angel,
Who stands the nearest to the Omniscient throne,
Knows but obedience: that his dearest pride,
His joy, his crown. While men—impatient men—
Fretting at aught that shackles their wild ways,
If but a moment's tangle thwart their path,
Which with a little patience might work clear,
Rush in, and with a sword of adamant
Cut the perplexing knot. Lead on! I follow. [*Exeunt.*

SCENE IV.—WESTMINSTER HALL.

People assembled; soldiers under COLONEL AXTELL, *who
has a thick stick in his hand.*

Axt. It is the hour. Now, men, be ready; and
when the King appears, shout one and all, Justice,
Justice! Execution, Execution! Do you hear?

Many voices. 'Aye, aye, aye. ·

Axt. Now shall you win a greater victory than Naseby. Only be firm! While the King lives, your necks are all in halters. Be firm! While he lives, plots, treasons, treacheries will have no end. All that ye have done will be undone. Freedom, Gospel, Glory, Cromwell, will be trodden into dust and perish.

Soldiers. Never!

Axt. Then stand firm, and cry, as you are bidden! Quit you as men : be strong!

A voice. God save the King!

Axt. Ha! Seize him! Where went he? Was it you? (*to a citizen.*)

Cit. Nay, Sir, not I.

Axt. Or you?

2nd Cit. Nay, Sir; do I look like it? I am all for——

Axt. What?

Cit. 'Sdeath, I cannot tell. There are so many changes from day to day, that an honest man, who has to get an honest living, doesn't know what to cry.

Axt.. Say, of what side are you?

Cit. I am for the side that's uppermost. I'm all for Cromwell. (*Soldiers applaud.*) Aye, that's the man. A clever rogue! There's no one like him.

Axt. Then shout, as I bid you, Justice, Justice!

2nd Cit. Justice, Justice!

Axt. Execution, execution!

2nd Cit. Execution, execution—of all knaves and rogues in England! (*Soldiers gather round him.*)

2nd Cit. I never said you were rogues. Lord! what

a thing is conscience! but look, here's the Court. Now
then—Justice !

Enter Judges, BRADSHAW *robed in red.*

Brad.   Call the names over.   You (*to a clerk*) draw
up the sentence.

> [*The names are called over, till interrupted at that
> of* FAIRFAX *by a woman's voice from the gallery,*
> 'He has too much wit to be here.' *The list
> completed, all sit down.*

Cromwell (*looking from a window in great agitation*).
My masters, he is come ; he is come : now are we about
the great work for which we have been called together.

Enter KING CHARLES, *guarded.*

K. Charles.   Sir, I shall ask to speak a word.   I hope
I shall not give you occasion to interrupt me——

Brad.   You shall answer in your turn : first listen to
the Court.

K. Charles.   Sir, by your favour, I desire to be heard.
But one word—an immediate judgment——

Brad.   Sir, you shall be heard in fit time ; you must
first hear the Court.

K. Charles.   Sir, I desire . . . what I have to say
concerns that judgment.   It is not easy, Sir, to recall a
hasty judgment.

Br.   You shall be heard, Sir, before sentence.
Gentlemen, it is known to you all that the prisoner at
the bar has been brought before the Court to answer a
charge of high treason, brought against him in·the name
of the people of England.

(*Voice from the gallery.*) It's a lie : not one-half of them. Where are they, or their consents? Oliver Cromwell is a traitor. (*Great disturbance.*)

Axt. Curse the she-devil! Shoot them——

A voice. It is Lady Fairfax. It is the General's wife.

Axt. Hold! She is gone again. Silence all!

Br. And yet in spite of all, though the charge be notorious, he will not answer to the charge. Nothing then remains but to pronounce his sentence, on which we are all agreed. (*To the King.*) Have you aught to say why sentence should not be pronounced?

K. Charles. I ask to be heard in the Painted Chamber by the Lords and Commons, on a matter of more importance to the peace of England and liberty of my subjects, than to my own preservation.

Several. What can he wish? 'Tis but to gain time. Will he abdicate? 'Tis but a trick.

The Soldiers. Justice! justice! Execution!

K. Charles. Hear me! Hear me! You are fouling justice at its source, when you refuse to hear me. Never was it known that a man, let alone a King, pleaded to be heard in an English Court of Justice, and his pleading was in vain.

Col. Downs. Are we men? or have we hearts of stone?

Crom. You will ruin the cause, and yourself.

Col. D. No matter, if I die for it, I must do it.

Crom. Colonel, are you mad? Can't you be quiet?

Col. D. No, Sir; I cannot be quiet. (*To Brad-shaw.*) My Lord, I have my reasons to give against this

H 2

sentence, and desire that the Court may adjourn to hear me.

Br. If anyone be not content, the Court must adjourn.   [*The Judges retire.*

Soldiers. No delay! No delay! We'll have his head! With the crown upon it! Off with him! off with him!

1st Sold. I lost a brother by your means. (*To the King.*)

2nd Sold. And I a father.

3rd Sold. Tell me, now, which is worth most, a king's head or a common man's.

[*They smoke in his face; adverse cries from the people; confusion.*

Re-enter the Judges.

Br. We cannot entertain your proposition.

K. Charles. Nay, surely; surely! an hour's delay. Is that so great a boon? Is everything new in England, that ye refuse me this?

Br. If you have no more to say, we will proceed to sentence.

K. Charles. I have no more to say. I am not used to plead, and ask in vain. All that I can or may say, is useless.

Br. 'Tis useless, aye! but what has made it so? Who is the cause of it? the bitter cause, Whence, as a fountain, all our miseries flow? Bear witness, Heaven! Be God the judge between us! Judge each of you, and all my countrymen, Through whom the guilt of this offending came!

We sought not war : we sought but to be free,
With chartered rights, beneath our native elms
To live and die peace loving Englishmen.
It might not be.   Thou didst compel us from it ;
Thou wert the first to unsheathe the civil sword,
The last to fling the broken blade away.
And in captivity (itself a sign
The God of battles had condemned thy cause),
Still set on treachery, thou didst plot revenge,
Still league with Irish, papists, foreigners,
All England's foes to war with England's weal,
From whom God's mercy only rescued us :
Yet feigning all the while to wish for peace.
Alas ! time was that what a monarch swore,
A people trusted.   Truth then answered truth :
And loyalty for love would tax itself
To sweat hard service for its loyal kings.
'Tis not so now : yet Heaven decide between us
Through whom the fatal first transgression came !
Therefore, since life craves life : so was it writ :
So is it writ still on our consciences :
Written in better books than those on paper,
Written in every honest Christian heart :
By all the blood thus wrongly shed for thee,
By widows' groanings, widows made by thee,
By kingly honour broken, trust betrayed,
And proffered peace, proffered in vain to thee,
By each, by all, we doom thee to the block,
We, England's people, doom thee, England's King,
And God have mercy on thy soul !   Remove him !

   K. Charles.   Sir, will you hear me a word ?

Br.   Sir, you are not to be heard after sentence.

K. Charles.   No?

Br.   No, Sir; by your leave: Guards, withdraw the prisoner!

K. Charles.   I may speak after sentence: by your leave, Sir——

Br.   Hold!

K. Charles.   The sentence.—I say, Sir, I do (*clamour*) I am not suffered to speak.   Expect what justice other people will now get, when ye will grant me none.   I die for the Church of England, and for her laws, bound up with the person of her King.

> [*One soldier cries ' God save your Majesty!'   An officer strikes him to the ground with a stick.*

K. Charles.   Poor fellow! the punishment exceeds the offence.   He does but say, what all but a few madmen feel.

> [*The soldiers again press round him, and blow tobacco in his face: spit at him : shout, ' Justice! Justice!'*

K. Charles.   Poor souls! for a piece of money they would do the same for their commanders.

> [*The people from behind cry, ' God save your Majesty!' ' God deliver you from your enemies!' Then he is taken away in a sedan chair, the bearers standing with their hats off, in spite of Axtell, who strikes them.   [Exeunt.*

ACT V.

SCENE I.—ROOM IN WHITEHALL.

Enter CROMWELL.

Crom.   It will be said, I did it, I alone,
For my own ends, not England's : and my name
(While meaner men rot in oblivion)
Will live as Jeroboam's, linked to shame
Through all the long hereafter.   [*A sound heard.*
                                              Ha, who calls
The name of Cromwell?   I can answer to it,
Can give each head, each count, each separate charge
That dooms the great delinquent.   I can meet him,
Sue and be sued before the great white Throne,
Nor dread the Eternal's verdict.   Speak, I dare thee,
Spirit or man !   No answer?   Then avaunt !
I know thee, tempter.   When great deeds are nigh,
Even in the thrilling hour of action's throes,
Thou lovest to wake, and whispering dark cold doubt
Here in the seat and bosom of resolve,
Blast hardihood, till even our bravest births
Die out in fear still-born.   The man must die.
'Tis his misfortune to be pinnacled
On that high place whence is no half-way fall :

Where men must be a blessing to be felt,
Or else must suffer.   And what's in a life,
In one poor life weighed with such mighty odds?
A grain of sand against a universe :
A single spark to all the stellar fires :
A sunmote to the glorious sun himself,
Joy of the earth and heaven.   O wherefore pause?
One foot in Canaan planted, wherefore turn
Back into bondage?   Hark ! the ages call :
The future beckons, and the distant years,
Big with the hopes of suffering Christendom,
Cheer us still onward.   Die then, Charles, and dead
Grant what thou grudgedst us living, set us free :
And root for ever out of English soil
The poisonous plant of godless tyranny.

Enter EPHRAIM, *roused by his loud voice.*

Ephraim.   Didst thou call, General?

Crom.   I called not.

Ephraim.   Methought——

Crom.   I called not.   Retire !   Or stay !   Are they
   come?

Ephraim.   Nay?

Crom.   That will do : they linger from the great
   work.

Ephraim (lingering).   Art thou well, General?

Crom.   The body is well, Ephraim : the body is well
enough.

Ephraim.   But the spirit sinketh.   The burden is
too heavy for thee.   In the old days thou hadst ever
a word of comfort or exhortation for the poor hungering

soul that sought thee : and in the battle thine eye was
as the sun of Ajalon, and thy coming was as the coming
of ten thousand.   But now thou hast a weary look : and
thou sighest often : and seekest to be alone.

   Crom.   Enough, good friend, enough !

   Ephraim.   Ah, General, it was better in those days :
it was better.   Then were we strong in the might of the
Lord, and waxed valiant in fight, and put to flight the
armies of the aliens.   But now these Courts, these
Councils, these carnal Ordinances, they suit not with
thee : they are not of the Lord.   Oh, General, quench
not the light of Israel !   Be careful of the life, in which
live all thy people : and suffer this folly, from one who
loves thee as his own soul.   Amen !   [*Exit.*

   Crom.   He loves me ; aye, and there be many that
hate me, and many envy.   Better was it in those old
days?   I know not.   But it was happier.   They tarry.
They linger from the great work.   Come then, Book of
Books, be thou my comfort, and my guide !

     (*He takes a Bible, and sits at a table with lamp ;
     then, after a pause,*)

I cannot read : the words rise up and mock me :
Nor think, so hurriedly the brain spins round,
Like bees in swarm-time.   O great God ! to hear
Those sweet, those heavenly voices once again,
That, whispering, erst did cheer me.   Dark, dark, dark !
Nothing but darkness ! and alone ! all lone !

     (*Buries his head in his hands : enter* MILTON,
     unobserved.)

   Milt.   Nay, not alone !

Crom. (*starting up.*) Who comes !   No   farther !
   Hold !

What, Milton ?

Milt.   Can I render aught of service ?

Crom.   Approach ! Thy hand ! Stand thus, and
   let me scan thee !

Dost thou approve ?

Milt.   What ?

Crom.   That, we do this day ?

Milt.   'Twas therefore that I came to greet thee,
   Cromwell.

Crom.   Yet many fall away, and leave me now.

My heart is heavy.

Milt.   What, on such a morn ?

Up, Cromwell, up !   This day a tyrant dies ;

A people's coronation dawns to-morrow :

And who but thou should wreath on freemen's brow

Freedom's fair crown ?

Crom.   I give them freedom, I ?

Milt.   Aye, freedom such as Heaven, not man doth
   will it,   .

Freedom with all her dangers, all her storms,

Restless and rude : now wrecking argosies,

Now wafting treasure-laden galleons in,

With all the largeness of her element.

Who freedom loves, loves earth's best gift of all :

It hath an inward virtue, which doth make

The free bare height richer than mines of gold :

But he who dreads the danger : he who feeds

A fat dull life, loving inglorious days,

Seeking not to be noble, but to be :
Hence, let him leave us ! Not for him the race,
Where Heaven's immortal garland may be won !
    Crom. Oh for a thousand spirits of pitch like thine !
    Milt. Nay spirits do but march, where spirits guide
    them :
We need thee, Cromwell. Righteousness and Truth
Sit on thy banner. As they call us on,
The God in us, the God within us swells
To greater victories ; be our leader still,
This time to more than Naseby's crowning charge,
And give us peace, Peace with her bloodless palm,
Peace with her sister Virtue undefiled !
More equal bid us grow ! the rich man's greatness
Set on a juster level with the poor ;
Each with enough, while none is surfeited !
Then let Religion from her height come down,
Doff her rich robe, and put Truth's plainness on ;
Rude sackcloth fits her better than the sheen
Of proud men's palaces. There sits she crowned,
The thunder from her prophet-lip uncurled,
Falsehearted, Delilah all smiles, within
Bemoaning virtue parted.
    Crom.   I have dreamed
Of such a task.
    Milt.   And Heaven shall make it true.
For whoso works with God, God works with him :
And, if he die, God takes his labour up :
And everliving helps his labour on,
Till fulness crown it in the perfect year.

Crom.   And England, when within her peace is sure,
Without——

Milt.   Her glory shall be terrible.

Crom.   How?

Milt.   She shall wake, as Samson, out of sleep—
The sleep that trammel'd strength did also nurse it—
Shake her invincible, her puissant locks,
And go forth armed.   God's enemies and hers
Shall quake before her.   Then in those great days,
The Spanish robber driven from off the main,
Ocean shall be her tributary.   Lands
Richer than Ophir, more remote than Ind,
Older than fame of legendary Nile,
Time's eldest, vassals to her youngest-born,
Shall own her sceptre.   She shall sit enthroned,
A commonalty overshadowing kings,
High among nations, loyal, temperate, free :
More great in praise of valour than old Rome,
Than Greece in civic wisdom. · From her loins
There shall spring empires.   Then to south and north,
Where round the world her belt of freedom stretches,
From tropic heats, and Nova-Zembla snows,
People and kings shall come in her chaste beams
Their fires to quench, or kindle.   She shall be
Mother of freedom : shield of the oppressed,
The oppressor's scourge : upon her glorious shore
Slaves drop their shackles, and are slaves no more.

Crom.   Ah, Milton, thou hast charmed my cloud
    away,
And Confidence resumes his former throne.
Now am I armed for all extremities.

But hark ! they come.   Leave me, and when again
My frenzy lowers, and all is dark around,
Then come, bright spirit, from the place of stars ;
Constant, while ,am tossed 'twīxt high and low !
Descend, and opening heaven to longing eyes,
Cheer my faint soul with airs of Paradise !
 Milt.   Only believe !   Who can believe, is strong.
 Crom.   'Tis hard.
 Milt.   But is't not harder to live on
Doubting ?   Beyond !   Oh, somewhere still beyond
Lies our great victory.   Farewell I farewell !
          [*Exit* MILTON.

 Enter IRETON, INGOLDSBY, HUNCKS, AXTELL, &c.

 1st Col.   Good morrow, General !
 Crom.   Good morrow, Sirs !
How fares the morning?
 2nd Col.   Rough and winterly.
The dark air glimmers white with drifting snow :
The ground is covering.
 Crom.   'Tis the better thus :
The fewer the spectators.
 Huncks.   And the more
The approvers of the deed.
 Crom.   How mean you, Sir?
 Huncks.   My mind misgives me, my Lord General.
 Crom.   On what ?
 Huncks.   The justice of our cause.
 Crom.   The justice ?
 Huncks.   Wherein is the King worse than us ?   If

he fought, we fought. If he plotted, we plotted. If he would willingly have fought again, so would we, if we had been beaten. If he sought friends everywhere, so should we, if we had known where to find them.

Crom. We friends with Irish, with Papists, with the Jesuit? Never! Why what a man is this, to strike sail just as we are coming into harbour. Sirrah, know you not that the King is the most hard-hearted man alive, and would hang us all up, like rotten scarecrows, if he had the power?

Huncks. Keep him then as an enemy in chains! not kill him as a murderer.

Crom. To plot against us under our very eyes, and if his hour come at last to regain his throne—pah! Is the man mad? At such a time to cry, Off! to leave us now at the great moment of all! Come, I know you, Colonel: I know you for a grumbler. You are one of those honest men who will always say, No, ere they will say you, Yes: who will find twenty faults in the little finger of a friend, not one flaw in the whole body of their enemies: you will be all for justice, so that justice break no bones: and will go far to bring a man's head to the block, providing there be no shedding of blood. Well, it is a merry fashion this grumbling: but now it is strangely out of season. Colonel, I tell you, all we ever did before, was as nothing to the present time. Here read this: 'tis the sentence, the King's sentence, and you shall sign it: now, ere you leave, you shall sign it.

' Whereas Charles Stuart, King of England, is and standeth convicted, attainted, and condemned of high treason, and other high crimes: and sentence upon

Saturday last was pronounced against him, to be put to death, by the severing of his head from his body : of which sentence execution yet remaineth to be done : these are therefore to will and require you to see the said sentence executed, in the open street, before Whitehall, upon Tuesday the 30th day of this instant month of January with full effect. And for so doing, this shall be your warrant. And these are to require all officers, and soldiers, and others the good people of England, to be assisting unto you in this service.'

> [*Gives him the pen : he stands irresolute.*

Crom. Sign !

Huncks. Never !

Crom. (*Holding him.*) Sign !

Huncks. I will not.

Crom. Sign, for the sake of England !

Huncks. Not for the whole world !

Crom. And is it with such as you that the Lord's battle is to be fought and won : lukewarm Laodiceans, neither hot nor cold for the great cause : half-hearted Sauls, who will spare Agag, though it has been said, Slay him, slay him ? Is it with you that we are to dig up this root of bitterness from the land, to make Zion to rejoice, and the Lord's people to be right glad ? Begone, Sirrah ! Your heart is not right in this matter. You shame yourself, you shame us all. This work must be done by truer men. Ha, Ingoldsby ; come hither ! You escaped me before : that shall you not again.

Ing. Nay, Cromwell, what need for me to sign ?

Crom. (*To* IRETON.) Hold fast there ! We have

him, if you let him not go. (*They make him sign. Then Cromwell daubs his face with ink.*)

Axtell. The General is merry this morning.

Iret. Fool, do you think men are always merry when they laugh? Why, there is more laughter in Bedlam than in all the world: where the poor fools laugh for very sadness of heart.

Crom. And now, my masters, now. See you this instrument? This shall be the death of one who was a bad King, who lived not for his people, but for himself: but with this will we make England free, and cause tyrants to tremble throughout the world. Take it with you, and—despatch! (*Exeunt all but Cromwell and Ireton.*)

Crom. They must be forced, forced, Ireten, to their good;
Like the dumb herd. Oh, who would govern men?

Iret. Nay, they are what the world is—naught but echoes.
Think not upon them!

Crom.   Think not! when my hand,
My own right hand, upon me turns the dagger,
Not think?

Iret.   'Twill pass.

Crom.   And leave us——

Iret.   Conquerors!

Crom. Ah, not of thee will it be writ hereafter,
He did this deed!

Iret.   How, Cromwell?

Crom.   Thou art safe,
Sheltered beneath the shield of Telamon.

Iret. Dost thou too doubt?

Crom.   I doubt not, but I feel.

Iret. It is too late.

Crom.   For what?

Iret.   To undo the deed.

Crom. Nay, think not that I wish the deed undone,
Were it thrice possible. 'Tis but a link,
One link in the eternal glorious chain,
That comes from God, and binding round the world
To God returns : nor in its horror more
Or less fore-ordered, than the balmy wind
That brings the rain, or sleeping infant's smile.
Only, who hears the order, his the call :
He must arise, and go, and do his work,
Oft with sad heart, oft with reluctant hands,
Not knowing what the Heavenly Master's plan,
More than the hodman, plying with his load,
Guesses what great cathedral's skyey dome
Works in the brain of its wise architect.

Iret. Then wherefore grieve?

Crom.   I know not, yet I grieve.
And he who does not is not more a man,
But less, a thing of stone.   Enough, no more !
So lie thou there, fell Hydra, crushed at last,
And crushed for ever !   Now this awe of tyrants,
Long-time through evil days our fathers' fear,
Our agony, shall grow henceforth a dream,
The unsubstantial fury of a dream,
To those born after : till our thankless heirs,
In weariness of freedom, sick for change,
Pygmies, the sons of giants, strange to wars,

Make cavil, and on chairs of silken ease,
E'en from the very vantage we had won,
Condemn their traitorous sires. Go! we are free.

                            [Exeunt.

SCENE II.—ROOM IN PALACE IN PARIS.

QUEEN HENRIETTA MARIA *and* LADY IN WAITING.

Queen. It is the day : it is the hour : they come not,
Where tarry ye, snail-footed messengers?
Had ye my reasons, ye would post with wings.
Hist, girl, d'ye see them?

Lady.   Some one slowly comes,
Leading his horse.

Queen.   At last, ah me, at last !

Lady. Reluctant, slow——

Queen.   He weary, and it lame !
Good horse, good rider!

Lady.   And he moves along
With downcast eyes——

Queen.   Belike he counts the stones
That keep him from me. Quick, bid him come up !

                          [Exit Lady.

How hard to wait, when but a single stair
Divides us from the tidings that we love !
Yet stay, downcast, reluctant, weary, slow,
Leading his horse! So comes not joyful news.
What if? But no—they cannot. O my husband !
Great God they dare not. Yet, oh had I striven
As much for peace, as I have spurred on war;

Had I but urged him (his great love was such,
He had denied me nothing) urged him, yield,
And bring me, not in triumph proudly home,
But throned in hearts ; true Queen of gentleness ;
Then—and had I those jewels set in pawn,
Not to feed war, new worlds array in arms,
To whet the brother's steel against the brother,
But to assuage war's wounds, to free the captive,
Cherish the orphan, and support the widow—
Oh then my heart had not been torn in twain,
Fearing a kingdom lost, a husband slain !
But hark ! they come : they come !

Enter LORD DIGBY, *and another.*

You are late, my lord ;
Give me the letters.   What ?   He turns away.
O heavens, my heart !   A knife !   This tedious string !
    [*Reading letter from the States' Ambassador.*
' It was in vain, Madam, that we pressed our suit
upon these cruel Englishmen.   Rock is not harder, snow
is not colder, than this man called, Cromwell.   We are
sorry to have progressed no better in what is our cause
as well as yours, and indeed the cause of all good persons
throughout the world.

' His execution (in grief we write it) is fixed for the
30th of January.'
    Queen.   To-day, perchance this hour !   O killing
        morn !   [*Faints.*
    Queen.   Air ! air ! more air !   Ye choke me.   What
        has happened ?

I 2

Who laid me here? Unhand me! Husband, Charles!
Oh I remember, murdered, murdered, murdered!
My dear lord murdered! Quick, why stand you here?
Neglectful lords! to the rescue! Die or save him!
Off! what, no movement? traitors!   [*They kneel.*

    Dig.   Madam, 'tis useless.

    Queen. To save him useless?

    Dig.   He must die to-day.

    Queen. Must—die—to-day! Must? Is there no
      help? None?

No, not to-day! It is so near, so near!
Do not say so! I am his wife. D'ye hear me?
His wife beloved and loving. Good, my lords!
Have pity on me! Oh you weep, you weep:
Within this bosom all Sahara burns:
And those sad drops but heat it hotter. See!
I go, I the chief lady in the land,
Will go, and barefoot weep from street to street,
From door to door, and kneel, and say such prayers,
That flinty and obdurate hearts shall yield,
And give him back to me. D'ye hear me? Quick!
Let us be going!

    Dig.   Madam!

    Queen.   Ah, why that word?

    Dig. It is too late.

    Queen.   Too late! What is too late?
Say, is not prayer swifter than any wing
Of swiftest Time? Cannot Heaven change these hearts,
These stubborn, stony, unrelenting hearts,
All in a moment? Oh, some respite! Life
Cut off in its sweet summer is not ripe
For eye of Heaven.

Dig.   Ah, Madam, riper grain
Was never garnered.   As a full-grown ear,
That being shook sheds blessing, so he moved,
So touched all hearts beholding.
    Queen.   How ?   You saw him ?
    Dig.   I did.
    Queen.   Where ?   When ?
    Dig.   Upon the trial-day
I stood and saw him borne to Westminster.
He enter'd in : no cap or feather stirred :
He stood, none rose : he sat, none bent the knee :
But blasphemous and scurril jests obscene
Pelted his ears : some demons spat on him
As once upon One greater, long before.
Yet he with sovereign air supremely calm
Kept his grand patience, like a King enthroned,
Whom princes bow their jewelled necks to honour :
Never a word he spake, nor flinched nor stirred :
But once or twice he sighed, as though in pity,
Men's hearts should be so hard.
    Queen.   And wept they not ?
Stones, stocks, fierce tigers, aught but fiercer men
Had wept to see him.   Had they no mothers, wives,
No tender-bodied daughters, no sweet babes,
Nothing to teach them arts of gentleness ?
Was nature dead in them, as they to nature,
That such sad sight should leave them all unmoved ?
But say, how looked he ?
    Dig.   Paler than of yore :
His eyes less proud, his hair with silver sprinkled,
Blanched ere its time with early-wintering snows.

And o'er him something awful, passing words,
Of sadness brooded, sadness not his own,
Not for himself; no passing trivial woe :
But the majestic grief of ruined kings,
Grief for the altar, prostrate with the throne,
The brawling hearth, the blood-stained sanctuary :
And for his people grief, surpassing all,
For all that's best laid lowest, the meanest raised :
Grief like the grief of God o'er fallen man,
Calm, uncomplaining, deep, immeasurable.

  Queen. 'Tis he : 'tis he : yet, oh ! 'tis he no longer.
Have you a letter from him?

  Dig.   Madam, none !
They would not suffer me to speak with him.

  Queen. Aye, churls are churls, and will be to the end :
Yet surely there was something in this sorrow
That might have touched the soul of churlishness.
Did you not plead with them?

  Dig.   'Twas all in vain.
They would not listen, barely hear, my prayer.

  Queen. In vain for wives to seek their dying lords !
In vain for husbands to console their wives !
In vain to sue to see a dying man,
To bring a living widow news of him !
Then is all vain. Vain love, vain courtesy !
Vain balm of kindness sovereign to abate
Harsh laws' sad venom ! Vain golden charity !
Let nothing henceforth live but fierce revenge,
To the last farthing strict, inexorable !
O sorrow, sorrow to be ever born !
And tenfold sorrow to be ever wed !

To wed a monarch sorrow worst of all !
For in the compass of one little night,
What trials come, what anguish, troops of fears,
To her that shares the weighty-metal'd crown !
Thenceforth farewell repose ! her couch is briars :
A thousand daggers pierce her in one life
Of him, her lord, sole aim and butt of all :
And separate daggers in a thousand lives
Of friends, of loved retainers for her slain.
O my dear lord ! my poor, poor murder'd lord !
So soon ! so soon !   Now even as I speak
The cruel moments into minutes grow ;
The cruel minutes hasten to the goal :
That goal is—Heaven : my heart denies to think
Of aught before that end, that goal of all.
Now take me hence.   Bring me a widow's weeds,
A wretched widow's saddest dreariest wear !
Off jewels, off, to hang on happier necks,
Once by a husband hung on happy me !
Lead me away : and Thou, the widow's friend,
Upbear my weakness !   Earth's sole prop is gone.

                                        [*Exeunt*

                    SCENE III.

CHARLES *asleep in prison; a stool, with a silver bell and*
    two watches on it, beside him; and silver basin, holding
    lamp. HERBERT *sleeping apart. Angels hover above,*
    singing.

                Sweeter far than Siren,
                    Heaven's blue deep along,
                Saint with Seraph quiring
                    Swell the Angelic song !

Pilgrims here ye wander,
  Slaves of hope and fear ;
Your true light is yonder,
  Shadows only here.

Here the night of sorrow,
  There the perfect day ;
Here delights that borrow
  Brightness from decay.

Here the pathway bleeding
  By affliction trod ;
There the gateway leading
  To the peace of God.

K. Charles (*waking*).   Methought I was in Heaven
  before my time,
And heard its songs of greeting, seraph-borne.
Stay, glorious vision, stay ! 'Tis gone, 'tis vanished,
As good things vanish, brief, while ill lives longer.
                                        [*Signs of dawn.*
But lo ! the light ! the morning breaks ; how slowly !
Slow, but inexorably sure it comes,
Like God's revenge !   Blest light, I cannot hate thee,
Though I have cause.   O faithless, he who set
'Twixt life and death, freedom or suffering on,
Refuses like a silly captive bird
To quit his wires, and, deaf to airs divine,
Mistrusts the liberty of boundless skies,
That woo him to their vast enfranchisement.
                                        [*A clock strikes.*
But hark, the hour ! It warns me. What, ho ! Herbert !
Herbert awake !   He sleeps : he dreams of trouble :
Poor soul, he has to live !   [*Going to him.*
  Her.   O my poor master !

K. Charles.   Poor! nay, why poor?   Rich with ex-
ceeding riches
Thou shouldst esteem me rather.
Her.   O my master!
K. Charles.   He bids thee wake.   [*Shaking him.*
Her.   Great heavens, methought I saw
The deadly axe fall on thee.
K. Charles.   Nay, I live
To need thy service, Herbert.   Tire me now
As for a wedding!   'Tis my spousal-morn,
My second spousal to my blessed Lord,
More glorious than my first one.
Her.   O that dream!
That horrible dream!   So long as life shall last
I see it—there!   Would it were all a dream!
Forgive me, Sire!
K. Charles.   Forgive thee!   Thanks, I'll wear
A second vest.   It freezes.   Flesh might creep,
And men affirm it was the spirit trembled.
But wherefore weep?
Her.   To see you, Sire, so calm.
K. Charles.   Nay, when the cup is drained to its last
drop,
Shall I for it show craven?   Trust me, friend,
An easy heart makes light of prison walls,
While conscience troubled can make dark a throne:
And I have known what 'tis—but that is over :
God judges not as man.   See there, who knocks?
Her.   Your children, Sire!

Enter the PRINCESS ELIZABETH, *the* DUKE *of* GLOUCESTER,
and BISHOP JUXON.

K. Charles.   Last drop of bitterness !
To say farewell !   Admit them, no one else !
Come hither, my sweet loves.   O children ! children!
Sweet mystery, our dearest joy, chief pain !
Jewels, that make the poor man's squalor shine
More than the childless splendour of a throne !
Who's rich in you is rich in all the world,
Who poor has nothing : nothing, though his wealth
More than outmatch the Indies.   [*Embraces them.*
                                   Bishop, you
Are welcome.   Yet one moment !
(*To Princess Eliz.*)   Know you, dears,
That I must die to-day ?
     Princess E.   O father, father !
     K. Charles.   Give me my jewels ! See, 'tis all the
          wealth
Left from a kingdom.   Take them, dear ones, take them'!
Share them between you !   And now mark my words !
My last, they must be few.   I charge thee, daughter,
Love God above all else, best love of all :
His Church the next, dear mother Church of England,
Set half-way twixt the pomps of erring Rome,
And starch'd Geneva's grim austerity.
Hold thou the middle way : avoid extremes !
And to thy brothers say (a dying man
Must bear no malice), say, I pardoned all
(So let them likewise), all my enemies.
But one thing more—thy mother—kiss her, child,

Say that I loved her, loved her to the last,
In death, as fond as on our wedding day,
Most dearly ever loved her : and in Heaven
I will, God willing, love her when she comes.
You will remember ?
    Princess E.   As my life, dear father.
I will remember it, and write it down,
And daily read it as a Holy Book,
Until I meet her.
    K. Charles.   Good ! so do, dear child !
And now time runs apace.   Come hither, son,
My little son.   Hark ! they will take my head,
Perhaps will make thee king : but mark me well,
Thou must not be a king before thy brothers :
Not while they live : though these hard men will kill
    them,
If they but catch them, and will kill thee last,
Cut off thine head too last.   Therefore I charge thee,
Never be made a king at all by them !
    Son.   I will be torn in pieces first.
    K. Charles.   I know it.
The lion's whelp will show his lion-blood,
E'en o'er the carcase of his sire.   God bless you !
Come to my heart, and let me feel you there,
Clasped once more in these arms !   O children, children,
Left friendless to the rude hate of the world,
What will become of you when I am gone ?
What will become of you ?
To-day I am a tower of mighty name,
Though fallen, a refuge from the pelting storm :
To-morrow, whatsoever ill befall,

I can do nothing for you.

Both. Father, stay !

K. Charles. Stay, oh how gladly ! but it may not
be :

There are some bad men in my kingdom, darlings,
Think 'twill be better for them, when I'm gone.
And they, not I, are masters. Fare you well !
The great good God, who loveth children, take you
Tenderly to His safe embracing arms,
And guard your youth, that should have been my care !
God bless you both, my children ! Fare you well !

                       [*They cling about him.*

What would you, darlings? Leave me, children, leave
me !

Both. Father, not yet!

K. Charles. And would you kill me here,
With your fond words, dear executioners ?

Both. Let us go with you !

K. Charles. Nay, not yet ! Not yet !
Sweet flowers, ye are not ripe for Paradise :
Bloom here a little longer ! Now one kiss,
And yet one more ! Another, and another !
O death, not dying is thy chiefest sting ;
'Tis, after thou art certain, living on
Those last few hours : it is the stripping oft
This life, this love, this vesture long endeared
Of old affection : 'tis from all we cherish
To part ; and in that moment's terrible plunge,
With the great tumbling breakers threatening doom,
Blackening to gulph us, see in fearful vision,
A thousand thousand times intensified,

'Neath the cross lightning's pale eye-withering glare,
The ruin, all the ruin we are leaving,
With those frail dear ones cowering on the wreck,
Whom the next wave may swallow.　Take them hence ! -
I have a work to do which the poor soul
Must do alone.　Farewell, sweet hearts, farewell !

> [*He goes to the window, leans against it in tears:
> then as they are leaving, rushes after them, em-
> braces them once more, then tears himself away;
> they go out weeping : he falls on his knees.*

K. Charles.　O Bishop, Bishop, lift my earthbound
soul !
I cannot lift it.

Bishop.　　　　　　　　Naked did we come
Into this world, and naked must we leave it.

K. Charles.　And we must weep.　'Tis nature's first
great law.

Bishop.　Look at this Cross !

K. Charles.　　　　　　My heart is blind with tears,
I cannot see it.

(Music sounds.)

Bishop.　Listen to yon strain
Now near, now far, as if some parent bird,
That takes a little flight, then comes again,
To tempt its young ones from their narrow home,
To wider joys in the clear firmament.

K. Charles.　The strain is outward : and my grief
within.
O my poor babes, my babes !

Bishop.　　　　　　　　He will protect them,
Who is a Father to the fatherless,

And takes the joyless widow to His care.

 K. Charles. Tyrannous men, how can ye such foul
  wrong?

 Bishop. Ah, Sire, forbear.

 K. Charles.   Would all mine enemies
Wrote all my evil doings in a book,
I would not shrink to wear it as a crown.

 Bishop. Patience, more gently! If for our faults alone
We endure buffets, 'tis small praise to bear them.
Merit is where having done all our best
We are beaten as the worst: to suffer causeless:
To bless being cursed: to pardon foully wronged:
This is the Christian's crown: his Master wore it:
Conquered, in this thou turnest to conqueror.

 K. Charles. To conqueror?

 Bishop.   Aye, more than conqueror!
For from the hour when thou shalt quit this life,
Suffering and martyred, Patience thy last work,
Patience, more mighty power than legions armed,
Shall 'gin her task, and creep from heart to heart,
Slowly instilling thy sad story in,
Till men shall grow enamoured in their turn
Of like obedience, and in simple faith
Renew old vows, welcome lost honour back,
And Time's rude stream run smoothly as before.

 K. Charles. You lift me upward.

 Bishop.   And for thine own self
Torn from this scene, Oh there the vision fades
Dying in ecstasy! What spirits feel,
Spirits only that can tell of. Our gross hearts
Earthfed know but earth's joys. Yet, Sire, believe me

Souls now on high in purest perfect bliss
Look back, and sufferings of the days of flesh
Fondly remember.   Those were glorious pains,
Pains of a joy in travail.   Through its cloud,
Lightly as one should lay a garment by,
A winter-robe, not needed of sweet Spring,
The creature rose, and soaring left behind
All that was not immortal.
 K. Charles.   Enough ! Enough !
More than enough of all that is not Heaven !
For now my soul is mounted to its height,
And from its skyey supernatural perch
O'erlooks the world.   False joy and sorrow hence !
Hence all concupiscent and vain desires !
How should a child, a heritor of Heaven,
Whose hope full-blossom'd flowers beyond the grave,
Grieve for earth's gauds, mere baubles of an hour,
Or fret his soul for muddy fields of clay,
Though joined together even to the utmost verge,
And all his own, his empire, his sole charge ?

 Enter COLONEL HACKER *and Guards, unseen by the*
       King.

Hence, I am free !   And you, my enemies,
Rather my friends, I call you friends who loose me
Beyond the changeful influence of the moon,
To things that change not : to the blessed feet
Of Him who died my sin to make His own,
His glory mine : with saint, and sinner shriven,
One joy, one song, one rapturous company,
Hymning the Great Eternal : for all this

I thank you, friends; and for your utmost wrong,
Your cruelest injury, wish you no more harm
Than that the tears ye dropped not on my sorrow,
Ye may have grace to pour upon yourselves.
Now, soul, for thy last work !   [*Kneels in prayer.*

   Hack. (*advancing*).   It is the time.

   Bishop.   Disturb him not : he prays.   He will not
     keep you.

How go we hence?

   Hack.   You, Sir?   I have no orders.

   Bishop.   Ye part us not.   I follow him to the grave.
Would I could follow farther !   But—he comes.

   K. Charles.   Sir, I could wish you a more pleasant
     service,

Though for myself ye cannot serve me more
Than by this summoning.   When shall we be gone?

   Hack.   At once, if't please you.

   K. Charles.   How go we?

   Hack.   Sire, on foot.

   K. Charles.   The better !   It will warm me to the work
On a cold morning.   Bishop, yet one more word.

                    [*They retire.*

My son, when I am gone, you must see him once
more, and tell him—it is my dying wish—tell him he
must not be king before his brothers.   Remember !

   Bishop.   I will do so, Sire.

   K. Charles.   Come, Herbert, leave me not till all is
     over !

   Herb.   My dear, dear Master !

   K. Charles.   Nay, no Master more !
But fellow-sufferer, sorrow's partner, peer,

Poorer than Job : yet from his deep of sorrow
Rising, a diver who has found his pearl,
To realms more radiant, suns more glorious, light
In Heaven, a joy eternal. Nay, dear friend,
Weeping ! Why weep? This is my triumph-morn,
And he who would my triumph's greatness share,
Must go with me apparelled in like hope,
And wear like bravery. For as for death,
With all its ugly and misshapen forms,
I mock at it. 'Tis but a juggler's show,
To scare weak souls, whose all is here below.

 Hack. Is it to death he goes, or to a wedding ?

 K. Charles. To both. Death is espousal to my Lord.
Now Sir !

 Hack. I pray you to forgive me, Sire.
My duty——

 K. Charles. Nay, if duty bid you to it,
You need not my forgiveness. Let us go ;
And not for all the kingdoms in the world,
Would I give up that bright, that better hope,
That calls me hence. My soul is up on high :
The flesh, impatient of its dreary load,
Pants to be free. See yonder is the way,
     [*A gleam of sunshine streams in.*
Heaven opens to me. I come., I leave behind
Earth, with its dead dark ball. O light most holy !
O God most mighty ! Ah I T'was slow in coming,
But being come, what rapture ! Life, farewell !

 (*Stands facing the light, with outstretched arms ; soldiers*
   come in ; funeral music heard ; then)

 K. Charles. Now !   [*Curtain falls.*

      K

SCENE IV.—BEFORE WHITEHALL.

Crowd, Soldiers, and Officers.

Officer. Keep back there : keep back! Use your pikes, men, if need be ! Keep back !

Woman (crying). Poor heart! poor heart! poor heart !

Sold. What mean you by that ' poor heart '?

Cit. 1. By your leave, sir, 'tis the opposite of a rich one.

Sold. She had best not say, ' Poor heart ' again.

Wom. Ah, dear me! dear me! God bless him ! God bless him !

Sold. Hold your tongue there, woman, or we'll cut it out for you !

Cit. 1. A good thing for her husband !

Cit. 2. Why may she not say, ' God bless him '?

Sold. You shall say nothing, sirrah, but what you are permitted to say.

2 *Sold.* That fellow has a mutinous look and tongue.

Cit. 1. May I not look as it pleases me ?

Sold. No, sir, you may not. 'Tis against orders. Move on there, move on!

Cit. 1. Come, let me do that for you ! Move on, good people, move on! Don't block up the King's highway !

Sold. What say you ?

Cit. 1. Why, then, the Parliament's highway. (*Soldier beats him.*) I mean the Army's highway ; or Oliver Crom-

well's highway ; or whose you please. (*Soldier seizes him.*)
Ha, look there, 'tis the Merry-andrew with his wares. Let
us hear him.   [*Enter Pedlar, who sings.*

> ' Oh yes, Oh yes, Oh yes,' I cry !
> Parliament wares, good people, buy !
> Parliament vests, all sorts and sizes,
> Buy, if you will, at easy prices :
> Many a storm and shower they'll bide,
> A world of knavery too they'll hide.

For you, sir ; for you, sir. (*Offering them : then to soldier
holding up an old sword.*) Here's an old sword ; very
rare and curious ; given by a master to his servant, and
used by that servant to stab his master withal ! Will you
buy, sir ? (*To another soldier, holding up a bottle.*) And
here's a more precious commodity than all. Here in
this phial are the true and exact tears of the crocodile,
brought by a lying Greek out of Egypt, and sold to a
Jew of Antioch, and by him brought into England now
for the first time. Will you buy, sir ? They are said to
be in much request in high places.

A voice. Take them to Oliver Cromwell.

Soldiers. Beat the knave ! beat him !

(*Bells toll; a deep groan from within the hall; drums
beat; enter people distractedly.*)

1*st Woman.* Ah, dear me, dear me ! I could not
have loved him more if he had been my own father.

2*nd Woman.* And I could not have believed it, if I
had not seen it with my own eyes. It's a sad day for
England, a sad day.

Cavalier in disguise (*lifting up his young son*). Boy,
listen to me. If you grow to be a man, see you take

K 2

vengeance for this day: mark me, vengeance for King Charles! Let no pleasure soften, no time make you forget! Let it be sweeter to you than love, dearer to you than gain, more vehement than hate, more awakening than loud-tongued honour! and may God forget you when you forget the murder of your King!

1st Woman. Neighbour Holdforth, you were near him on the scaffold. What said he about the axe?

Hold. He said, do not hurt the axe! do not hurt it!

2nd Woman. Aye, poor man! He wished to make an end quickly.

1st Woman. And what said he to the bishop? It seemed barely a word; but O his face, his face, as he said it!

Hold. He said, Remember!

1st Woman. Remember. Remember what?

Hold. Why, to be sure, remember all the good things he'd been saying to him before.

Cavalier. Remember! his dying word! Oh, my master! 'Tis the watchword for all true hearts in England during this night of terror. When we remember not, then let us cease to be. Boy, do you hear? Remember!

Many voices. God bless him! God bless bim!

[*Bells toll faster.*

Cries of- -Here it comes!

SCENE V.

The King's coffin is borne in, preceded by Bishop Juxon reading the Burial Service from the Prayer Book: an Officer puts his hand upon the page.

Bishop. Why this interruption, sir?

Off. That book is forbidden. You may not bury him with that book.

Bishop. So you have done your duty, sir. If it please you, retire. [*Officer withdraws.*

Bishop. So let him pass unhonoured to the tomb!
He needs no supplication to commend him,
Where he is going. There all is freshly heard:
Witness, Recorder, verdict, all are new:
And in that Final Court of great Appeal
Victim and judge do often change their places,
Who sentenced, now condemned. Thither he goes,
To that tribunal, there to plead his cause
In Truth's own ears, from wrong to Justice' self,
From injury on earth to right in heaven:
From lawless man to perfect law of God.
(*The people sweep in, and drive soldiers back; the coffin
advances, snow falling.*)[8]
Set down the coffin here in sight of Heaven,
And let white angels scatter snow upon it,
Not whiter than his innocence! O Judgment!
Allseeing eye! whose lightnings scour the world,
Who takest note if but a sparrow fall,
And numberest our hairs' integrity,

[8] See Appendix.

Where wert Thou when this bloody deed was done,
Dread Power, where wert thou? Peace! What words
    are these?
Can his great patience (there it was he shone
More than in all his greatness) teach me nothing
But wild rebellion? 'Tis the will of Heaven,
And Heaven has far-off meanings, which, as stars,
Not of our sphere, in distant skies unknown,
Shoot yearning down to greet a sister-world,
Somewhen to flash in radiance on our sight.
Dread Power, we trust thee. Rest then noble heart,
Old, not in years, but anguish! Rest at last,
Grey head, discrowned, dishonoured, yet in dust,
Even in the dust, more sovereign lord of all,
More king of hearts, than in thy ruling hour,
Lip-honoured, in the pomp of all thy pride!
Rest, thou hast conquered! Suffering now is over:
Rancour, abating from its torrent-height,
Shall come, and murmur requiems round thy tomb,
There sowing flowers, where late it hoarsely raged:
Hatred shall grow remorse, revenge regret:
While from all parts—for all shall hear thy fame
And love it—pilgrims shall embrace the earth
Where thou didst fall: yea, kiss the sacred dust,
Blest dust, ennobled with thy blood for ever;
Happy, if they may bear some grain away,
Dear relic of their master's martyrdom.
                        [*Cries from the people.*
Nay, men of England, do not weep for him!
Weep for yourselves! He is at peace: his failings,
Born of the flesh, die with it: his great virtues,

That were the spirit's, mounting with it, shine
A glory greater than of sun and moon,
In Heaven a sign everlasting.   Go your ways!
Follow the light! press where it points you on!
And when your hour comes to confess and suffer,
Or falsely live lapped in inglorious ease,
Then, though all interest lure you to the wrong,
And kind concealment cover up the wronger;
Though custom gloze and varnish o'er the deed,
And men, like sinners, smile upon the doer;
I charge you by the memory of this day,
This awful day, whereon a king did perish,
Slain by his subjects for the truth he honoured,
Like him endure! be faithful!   Like him live,
Though others all belie themselves, the life
Ye deem the highest! and, if it need be choose
'Twixt honest death and shameful living, joy
To die like him a martyr!   Bearers, rise!
Move on slow pomp, and ever as we move
Toll bells, ring dirges, blasts of winter rave,
While England's best is passing to his grave!

CURTAIN FALLS.

APPENDIX.

Note 1. Page 9.

This characteristic remark of the Queen's about Strafford may be found in Strickland's *Queens of England*, vol. v. p. 271. 'Strafford was ugly, but agreeable enough in person, and had the finest hands in the world.'

Note 2. Page 39.

See Guizot's *History of the English Revolution*' (Translation), p. 354. ' " For the rest," he added, " I alone understand my position ; be quite easy as to the concessions which I may grant ; when the time comes, I shall very well know how to treat these rogues, and instead of a silken garter, I will fit them with a hempen halter." The two generals looked at each other, and, all their suspicions thus confirmed, returned to Windsor.'

Note 3. Page 46.

There was a form of service in the Prayer-book at this time, for touching for the King's Evil, and it is found as late as 1719. Kings of the House of Brunswick never put the supposed power to the proof. Indeed, Jacobites asserted that it died out with the Stuarts, though surviving in Charles Edward at Holyrood in 1745.

Note 4. Page 61.

See Guizot, p. 410. ' " Like Moses," said Hugh Peters to the generals, in a sermon before the remnant of the two Houses,' &c.

Note 5.   Page 72.

Fairfax's position at this time, considering his high character, is
one of the inexplicable things of history. He disapproved of the
execution of the King ; he would not sit upon the Commission that
tried him ; his brave wife's solitary protest at the trial is known to
all ; and yet he continued to hold his office as General of the Army
of the Parliament, leaving Cromwell to run his course unchecked.

Note 6.   Page 77.

See *Biographical Dictionary* (Chalmers'), article ' Cromwell,'
p. 53.

' Colonel John Cromwell, an officer in the service of Holland,
was sent over (when the news of the King's trial arrived there) with
letters credential from the States, to which was added a blank with
the King's signet, and another of the Prince's, both confirmed by the
States, for Cromwell to set down his own conditions if he would
save his Majesty's life.

' The Colonel went to his kinsman's house, and began with much
freedom to set before him the heinousness of the act then about to
be committed, and the detestation with which it was regarded
abroad ; and reminded him of his former words about the King.
To this Cromwell answered that times were now altered, &c.

    .   .   .   .

' Upon this the Colonel stepped back and suddenly shut the door,
which made Cromwell apprehend he was going to be assassinated :
but pulling out his papers, he said to him, " Cousin, see here ; it is
now in your power to make yourself and your family honourable for
ever : otherwise, as they changed their name before from Williams
to Cromwell, so now they must be forced to change it again : for
this will bring such ignominy upon the whole generation of them,
as no time will be able to deface." At this Cromwell paused a
little,' &c. &c.

See also Guizot, p. 422.   ' Already John Cromwell,' &c.

Note 7.   Page 84.

There was a tradition (cf. Strickland's *Queens of England*, vol.
v. p. 385) that the wife of Cromwell shared in the general grief for
the murder of the King.

See also Clarendon, *History of Rebellion*, Book xv., paragraph

145, as showing the tone of mind of Mrs. Claypole, Cromwell's favourite daughter.

'And though nobody was near enough to hear the particulars [of what Mrs. Claypole said to him on her death-bed], yet her often mentioning, in the pains she endured, the blood her father had spilt, made people conclude that she had presented his worst actions to his consideration.'

Carlyle. *Cromwell's Letters and Speeches*, vol. i. p. 93, note 6, calls this 'fudge,' but does not give his reasons.

Note 8.   Page 133.

The fall of snow really took place during the King's subsequent funeral at Windsor.

LONDON : PRINTED BY

SPOTTISWOODE AND CO., NEW-STREET SQUARE

AND PARLIAMENT STREET

GENERAL LIST OF WORKS

PUBLISHED BY

Messrs. LONGMANS, GREEN, and CO.

PATERNOSTER ROW, LONDON.

——o○}○{○o——

History, Politics, Historical Memoirs, &c.

JOURNAL of the **REIGNS** of **KING GEORGE IV.** and **KING WILLIAM IV.** By the late CHARLES C. F. GREVILLE, Esq. Edited by HENRY REEVE, Esq. Fifth Edition. 3 vols. 8vo. 36s.

RECOLLECTIONS and SUGGESTIONS, 1813-1873. By JOHN Earl RUSSELL, K.G. New Edition, revised and enlarged. 8vo. 16s.

The **HISTORY of ENGLAND** from the Fall of Wolsey to the Defeat of the Spanish Armada. By JAMES ANTHONY FROUDE, M.A. late Fellow of Exeter College, Oxford.

> LIBRARY EDITION, Twelve Volumes, 8vo. price £8. 18s.
> CABINET EDITION, Twelve Volumes, crown 8vo. price 72s.

The **ENGLISH in IRELAND** in the **EIGHTEENTH CENTURY.** By JAMES ANTHONY FROUDE, M.A. late Fellow of Exeter College, Oxford. 3 vols. 8vo. price 48s.

The **HISTORY of ENGLAND** from the Accession of James the ond. By Lord MACAULAY.

> STUDENT'S EDITION, 2 vols. crown 8vo. 12s.
> PEOPLE'S EDITION, 4 vols. crown 8vo. 16s.
> CABINET EDITION, 8 vols. post 8vo. 48s.
> LIBRARY EDITION, 5 vols. 8vo. £4.

LORD MACAULAY'S WORKS. Complete and Uniform Library Edition. Edited by his Sister, Lady TREVELYAN. 8 vols. 8vo. with Portrait price £5. 5s. cloth, or £8. 8s. bound in tree-calf by Rivière.

On **PARLIAMENTARY GOVERNMENT** in **ENGLAND**; Its Origin, Development, and Practical Operation. By ALPHEUS TODD, Librarian of the Legislative Assembly of Canada. 2 vols. 8vo. price £1. 17s.

The **CONSTITUTIONAL HISTORY** of **ENGLAND**, since the Accession of George III. 1760—1860. By Sir THOMAS ERSKINE MAY, C.B. The Fourth Edition, thoroughly revised. 3 vols. crown 8vo. price 18s.

DEMOCRACY in **EUROPE**; a History. By Sir THOMAS ERSKINE MAY, K.C.B. 2 vols. 8vo. [*In the press.*]

The **NEW REFORMATION**, a Narrative of the Old Catholic Movement, from 1870 to the Present Time; with an Historical Introduction. By THEODORUS. 8vo. price 12s.

A

The **OXFORD REFORMERS** — John Colet, Erasmus, and Thomas More ; being a History of their Fellow-work. By FREDERIC SEEBOHM. Second Edition, enlarged. 8vo. 14s.

LECTURES on the **HISTORY** of **ENGLAND**, from the Earliest Times to the Death of King Edward II. By WILLIAM LONGMAN, F.S.A. With Maps and Illustrations. 8vo. 15s.

The **HISTORY** of the **LIFE** and **TIMES** of **EDWARD** the **THIRD**. By WILLIAM LONGMAN, F.S.A. With 9 Maps, 8 Plates, and 16 Woodcuts. 2 vols. 8vo. 28s.

INTRODUCTORY LECTURES on **MODERN HISTORY**. Delivered in Lent Term, 1842 ; with the Inaugural Lecture delivered in December 1841. By the Rev. THOMAS ARNOLD, D.D. 8vo. price 7s. 6d.

WATERLOO LECTURES ; a Study of the Campaign of 1815. By Colonel CHARLES C. CHESNEY, R.E. Third Edition. 8vo. with Map, 10s. 6d.

HISTORY of **ENGLAND** under the **DUKE** of **BUCKINGHAM** and CHARLES the FIRST, 1624-1628. By SAMUEL RAWSON GARDINER, late Student of Ch. Ch. 2 vols. 8vo. with two Maps, price 24s.

The **SIXTH ORIENTAL MONARCHY**; or, the Geography, History, and Antiquities of Parthia. By GEORGE RAWLINSON, M.A. Professor of Ancient History in the University of Oxford. Maps and Illustrations. 8vo. 16s.

The **SEVENTH GREAT ORIENTAL MONARCHY**; or, a History of the Sassanians : with Notices, Geographical and Antiquarian. By G. RAWLINSON, M.A. Professor of Ancient History in the University of Oxford. 8vo. with Maps and Illustrations.   [In the press.

A **HISTORY** of **GREECE**. By the Rev. GEORGE W. COX, M.A. late Scholar of Trinity College, Oxford. VOLS. I. & II. (to the Close of the Peloponnesian War). 8vo. with Maps and Plans, 36s.

GENERAL HISTORY of **GREECE** to the Death of Alexander the Great. By the Rev. GEORGE W. COX, M.A. late Scholar of Trinity College, Oxford; Author of 'The Aryan Mythology' &c. Crown 8vo.   [In the press.

GREEK HISTORY from Themistocles to Alexander, in a Series of Lives from Plutarch. Revised and arranged by A. H. CLOUGH. New Edition. Fcp. with 44 Woodcuts, 6s.

The **TALE** of the **GREAT PERSIAN WAR**, from the Histories of Herodotus. By GEORGE W. COX, M.A. New Edition. Fcp. 3s. 6d.

The **HISTORY** of **ROME**. By WILLIAM IHNE. VOLS. I. and II. 8vo. price 30s. The Third Volume is in the press.

GENERAL HISTORY OF ROME from the Foundation of the City to the Fall of Augustulus, B.C. 753—A.D. 476. By the Very Rev. C. MERIVALE, D.D. Dean of Ely. With Five Maps. Crown 8vo. 7s. 6d.

HISTORY of the **ROMANS** under the **EMPIRE**. By the Very Rev. C. MERIVALE, D.D. Dean of Ely. 8 vols. post 8vo. 48s.

The **FALL** of the **ROMAN REPUBLIC** ; a Short History of the Last Century of the Commonwealth. By the same Author. 12mo. 7s. 6d.

The **STUDENT'S MANUAL** of the **HISTORY** of **INDIA**, from the Earliest Period to the Present. By Colonel MEADOWS TAYLOR, M.R.A.S. M.R.I.A. Second Thousand. Crown 8vo. with Maps, 7s. 6d.

The **HISTORY** of **INDIA**, from the Earliest Period to the close of Lord Dalhousie's Administration. By J. C. MARSHMAN. 3 vols. crown 8vo. 22s. 6d.

The **NATIVE STATES** of **INDIA** in **SUBSIDIARY ALLIANCE**
with the BRITISH GOVERNMENT; an Historical Sketch. With a Notice of
the Mediatized and Minor States. By Colonel G. B. MALLESON, C.S.I. Guardian
to His Highness the Mahárájá of Mysore. With 6 Coloured Maps. 8vo. 15s.

INDIAN POLITY; a View of the System of Administration in India.
By Lieutenant-Colonel GEORGE CHESNEY, Fellow of the University of Calcutta.
New Edition, revised; with Map. 8vo. price 21s.

The **IMPERIAL** and **COLONIAL CONSTITUTIONS** of the **BRI-**
TANNIC EMPIRE, including INDIAN INSTITUTIONS. By Sir EDWARD
CREASY, M.A. With 6 Maps. 8vo. price 15s.

HISTORY of the **REPUBLIC** of **FLORENCE.** Translated from the
Italian of the Marchese GINO CAPPONI by SARAH FRANCES ALLEYNE. 2 vols.
8vo. [In the press.

STUDIES from **GENOESE HISTORY.** By Colonel G. B. MALLESON,
C.S.I. Guardian to His Highness the Mahárájá of Mysore. Crown 8vo. 10s. 6d.

CRITICAL and **HISTORICAL ESSAYS** contributed to the *Edinburgh
Review.* By the Right Hon. LORD MACAULAY.

CHEAP EDITION, authorised and complete. Crown 8vo. 3s. 6d.

CABINET EDITION, 4 vols. post 8vo. 24s.	LIBRARY EDITION, 3 vols. 8vo. 36s.
PEOPLE'S EDITION, 2 vols. crown 8vo. 8s.	STUDENT'S EDITION, 1 vol. cr. 8vo. 6s.

HISTORY of **EUROPEAN MORALS,** from Augustus to Charlemagne
By W. E. H. LECKY, M.A. Second Edition. 2 vols. 8vo. price 28s.

HISTORY of the **RISE** and **INFLUENCE** of the **SPIRIT** of
RATIONALISM in EUROPE. By W. E. H. LECKY, M.A. Cabinet Edition,
being the Fourth. 2 vols. crown 8vo. price 16s.

The **HISTORY** of **PHILOSOPHY,** from Thales to Comte. By
GEORGE HENRY LEWES. Fourth Edition. 2 vols. 8vo. 32s.

The **HISTORY** of the **PELOPONNESIAN WAR.** By THUCYDIDES.
Translated by R. CRAWLEY, Fellow of Worcester College, Oxford. 8vo. 21s.

The **MYTHOLOGY** of the **ARYAN NATIONS.** By GEORGE W.
Cox, M.A. late Scholar of Trinity College, Oxford, 2 vols. 8vo. 28s.

TALES of **ANCIENT GREECE.** By GEORGE W. COX, M.A. late
Scholar of Trin. Coll. Oxon. Crown 8vo. price 6s. 6d.

HISTORY of **CIVILISATION** in England and France, Spain and Scot-
land. By HENRY THOMAS BUCKLE. New Edition of the entire Work, with
a complete INDEX. 3 vols. crown 8vo. 24s.

SKETCH of the **HISTORY** of the **CHURCH** of **ENGLAND** to the
Revolution of 1688. By the Right Rev. T. V. SHORT, D.D. Lord Bishop of
St. Asaph. Eighth Edition. Crown 8vo. 7s. 6d.

MAUNDER'S HISTORICAL TREASURY; General Introductory Outlines of Universal History, and a series of Separate Histories. Latest Edition,
revised by the Rev. G. W. Cox, M.A. Fcp. 8vo. 6s. cloth, or 10s. calf.

CATES' and **WOODWARD'S ENCYCLOPÆDIA** of **CHRONOLOGY,**
HISTORICAL and BIOGRAPHICAL; comprising the Dates of all the Great
Events of History, including Treaties, Alliances, Wars, Battles, &c.; Incidents
in the Lives of Eminent Men and their Works, Scientific and Geographical Discoveries, Mechanical Inventions, and Social Improvements. 8vo. price 42s.

The **HISTORICAL GEOGRAPHY** of **EUROPE.** By E. A. FREEMAN,
D.C.L. late Fellow of Trinity College, Oxford. 8vo. Maps. [In the press.

The **ERA** of the **PROTESTANT REVOLUTION.** By F. SEEBOHM.
With 4 Coloured Maps and 12 Diagrams on Wood. Fcp. 8vo. 2s. 6d.

A 2

The **CRUSADES**   By the Rev. G. W. Cox, M.A. late Scholar of Trinity College, Oxford. With Coloured Map. Fcp. 8vo. 2s. 6d.

The **THIRTY YEARS' WAR, 1618-1648.** By Samuel Rawson Gardiner, late Student of Christ Church. With Coloured Map. Fcp. 8vo. 2s. 6d.

The **HOUSES of LANCASTER and YORK;** with the Conquest and Loss of France. By James Gairdner, of the Public Record Office. With Five Coloured Maps. Fcp. 8vo. 2s. 6d.

EDWARD the THIRD. By the Rev. W. Warburton, M.A. late Fellow of All Souls College, Oxford. With 3 Coloured Maps and 8 Genealogical Tables. Fcp. 8vo. 2s. 6d.

REALITIES of IRISH LIFE. By W. Steuart Trench, late Land Agent in Ireland to the Marquess of Lansdowne, the Marquess of Bath, and Lord Digby. Cheaper Edition. Crown 8vo. price 2s. 6d.

Biographical Works.

AUTOBIOGRAPHY. By John Stuart Mill. 8vo. price 7s. 6d.

The **LIFE and LETTERS of LORD MACAULAY.** By his Nephew, G. Otto Trevelyan, M.P. 2 vols. 8vo.   [In the press.

ADMIRAL SIR EDWARD CODRINGTON, a Memoir of his Life; with Selections from his Private and Official Correspondence. Abridged from the larger work, and edited by his Daughter, Lady Bourchier. With Portrait, Maps, &c. Crown 8vo. 7s. 6d.

The **LIFE of NAPOLEON III.** derived from State Records, Unpublished Family Correspondence, and Personal Testimony. By Blanchard Jerrold. 4 vols. 8vo. with numerous Portraits and Facsimiles. Vols. I. and II. price 18s. each. The Third Volume is in the press.

LIFE and LETTERS of Sir GILBERT ELLIOT, First EARL of MINTO. Edited by the Countess of Minto. 3 vols. 8vo. 31s. 6d.

ESSAYS in MODERN MILITARY BIOGRAPHY. By Charles Cornwallis Chesney, Lieutenant-Colonel in the Royal Engineers. 8vo. 12s. 6d.

The **MEMOIRS of SIR JOHN RERESBY,** of Thrybergh, Bart. M.P. for York, &c. 1634-1689. Written by Himself. Edited from the Original Manuscript by James J. Cartwright, M.A. 8vo. price 21s.

ISAAC CASAUBON, 1559-1614. By Mark Pattison, Rector of Lincoln College, Oxford. 8vo. 18s.

BIOGRAPHICAL and CRITICAL ESSAYS, reprinted from Reviews, with Additions and Corrections. Second Edition of the Second Series. By A. Hayward, Q.C. 2 vols. 8vo. price 28s. Third Series, in 1 vol. 8vo. price 14s.

LORD GEORGE BENTINCK; a Political Biography. By the Right Hon. Benjamin Disraeli, M.P. Crown 8vo. price 6s.

The **LIFE OF ISAMBARD KINGDOM BRUNEL,** Civil Engineer. By Isambard Brunel, B.C.L. With Portrait, Plates, and Woodcuts. 8vo. 21s.

RECOLLECTIONS of PAST LIFE. By Sir Henry Holland, Bart. M.D. F.R.S. late Physician-in-Ordinary to the Queen. Third Edition. Post 8vo. price 10s. 6d.

The **LIFE and LETTERS of the Rev. SYDNEY SMITH.** Edited by his Daughter, Lady Holland, and Mrs. Austin. Crown 8vo. price 2s. 6d.

LEADERS of PUBLIC OPINION in IRELAND; Swift, Flood, Grattan, and O'Connell. By W. E. H. LECKY, M.A. New Edition, revised and enlarged. Crown 8vo. price 7s. 6d.

DICTIONARY of GENERAL BIOGRAPHY; containing Concise Memoirs and Notices of the most Eminent Persons of all Countries, from the Earliest Ages. By W. L. R. CATES. New Edition, extended in a Supplement to the Year 1875. Medium 8vo. price 25s. The SUPPLEMENT (comprising 502 additional Notices and Memoirs) separately, price 4s. 6d.

The OFFICIAL BARONAGE of ENGLAND, Shewing the Offices and Honours held by every Peer from 1065 to 1875; also the Personal Characteristics of each, their Armorial Bearings, Family Colours, Badges, and Mottoes. With more than 1,200 Illustrations (Portraits, Effigies, Shields of Arms, and Antographs). By JAMES E. DOYLE. Fcp. 4to.   [In the press.

LIFE of the DUKE of WELLINGTON. By the Rev. G. R. GLEIG, M.A. Popular Edition, carefully revised; with copious Additions. Crown 8vo. with Portrait, 5s.

FELIX MENDELSSOHN'S LETTERS from *Italy and Switzerland,* and *Letters from* 1833 *to* 1847, translated by Lady WALLACE. New Edition, with Portrait. 2 vols. crown 8vo. 5s. each.

MEMOIRS of SIR HENRY HAVELOCK, K.C.B. By JOHN CLARK MARSHMAN. Cabinet Edition, with Portrait. Crown 8vo. price 3s. 6d.

VICISSITUDES of FAMILIES. By Sir J. BERNARD BURKE, C.B. Ulster King of Arms. New Edition, remodelled and enlarged. 2 vols. crown 8vo. 21s.

The RISE of GREAT FAMILIES, other Essays and Stories. By Sir J. BERNARD BURKE, C.B. Ulster King of Arms. Crown 8vo. price 12s. 6d.

ESSAYS in ECCLESIASTICAL BIOGRAPHY. By the Right Hon. Sir J. STEPHEN, LL.D. Cabinet Edition. Crown 8vo. 7s. 6d.

MAUNDER'S BIOGRAPHICAL TREASURY. Latest Edition, reconstructed, thoroughly revised, and in great part rewritten; with 1,000 additional Memoirs and Notices, by W. L. R. CATES. Fcp. 8vo. 6s. cloth; 10s. calf.

LETTERS and LIFE of FRANCIS BACON, including all his Occasional Works. Collected and edited, with a Commentary, by J. SPEDDING, Trin. Coll. Cantab. Complete in 7 vols. 8vo. £4. 4s.

The LIFE, WORKS, and OPINIONS of HEINRICH HEINE. By WILLIAM STIGAND. 2 vols. 8vo. with Portrait of Heine, price 28s.

Criticism, Philosophy, Polity, &c.

The LAW of NATIONS considered as INDEPENDENT POLITICAL COMMUNITIES; the Rights and Duties of Nations in Time of War. By Sir TRAVERS TWISS, D.C.L., F.R.S. New Edition, revised; with an Introductory Juridical Review of the Results of Recent Wars, and an Appendix of Treaties and other Documents. 8vo. 21s.

CHURCH and STATE: their relations Historically Developed. By T. HEINRICH GEFFCKEN, Professor of International Law at the University of Strasburg. Translated from the German by E. FAIRFAX TAYLOR. [In the press.

A SYSTEMATIC VIEW of the SCIENCE of JURISPRUDENCE. By SHELDON AMOS, M.A. Professor of Jurisprudence to the Inns of Court, London. 8vo. price 18s.

A PRIMER of the ENGLISH CONSTITUTION and GOVERNMENT.
By SHELDON AMOS, M.A. Professor of Jurisprudence to the Inns of Court.
Second Edition, revised. Crown 8vo. 6s.

The INSTITUTES of JUSTINIAN; with English Introduction, Translation and Notes. By T. C. SANDARS, M.A. Sixth Edition. 8vo. 18s.

SOCRATES and the SOCRATIC SCHOOLS. Translated from the German of Dr. E. ZELLER, with the Author's approval, by the Rev. OSWALD J. REICHEL, M.A. Crown 8vo. 8s. 6d.

The STOICS, EPICUREANS, and SCEPTICS. Translated from the German of Dr. E. ZELLER, with the Author's approval, by OSWALD J. REICHEL, M.A. Crown 8vo. price 14s.

The ETHICS of ARISTOTLE, with Essays and Notes. By Sir A. GRANT, Bart. M.A. LL.D. Third Edition. 2 vols. 8vo. 32s.

The POLITICS of ARISTOTLE; Greek Text, with English Notes. By RICHARD CONGREVE, M.A. New Edition, revised. 8vo. 18s.

The NICOMACHEAN ETHICS of ARISTOTLE newly translated into English. By R. WILLIAMS. B.A. Fellow and late Lecturer of Merton College, and sometime Student of Christ Church, Oxford. 8vo. 12s.

PICTURE LOGIC; an Attempt to Popularise the Science of Reasoning by the combination of Humorous Pictures with Examples of Reasoning taken from Daily Life. By A. SWINBOURNE, B.A. With Woodcut Illustrations from Drawings by the Author. Second Edition. Fcp. 8vo. price 5s.

ELEMENTS of LOGIC. By R. WHATELY, D.D. late Archbishop of Dublin. New Edition. 8vo. 10s. 6d. crown 8vo. 4s. 6d.

Elements of Rhetoric. By the same Author. New Edition. 8vo. 10s. 6d. crown 8vo. 4s. 6d.

English Synonymes. By E. JANE WHATELY. Edited by Archbishop WHATELY. Fifth Edition. Fcp. 8vo. price 3s.

On the INFLUENCE of AUTHORITY in MATTERS of OPINION. By the late Sir GEORGE CORNEWALL LEWIS, Bart. New Edition. [Nearly ready.

DEMOCRACY in AMERICA. By ALEXIS DE TOCQUEVILLE. Translated by HENRY REEVE, Esq. New Edition. 2 vols. crown 8vo. 16s.

ORDER and PROGRESS: Part I. Thoughts on Government; Part II. Studies of Political Crises. By FREDERIC HARRISON, M.A. of Lincoln's Inn. 8vo. price 14s.

COMTE'S SYSTEM of POSITIVE POLITY, or TREATISE upon SOCIOLOGY. Translated from the Paris Edition of 1851–1854, and furnished with Analytical Tables of Contents. In Four Volumes, 8vo. each forming in some degree an independent Treatise :—

VOL. I. General View of Positivism and its Introductory Principles. Translated by J. H. BRIDGES, M.B. Price 21s.

VOL. II. Social Statics, or the Abstract Laws of Human Order. Translated by F. HARRISON, M.A. Price 14s.

VOL. III. Social Dynamics, or the General Laws of Human Progress (the Philosophy of History). Translated by E. S. BEESLY, M.A. [In the press.

VOL. IV. Synthesis of the Future of Mankind. Translated by R. CONGREVE, M.D.; and an Appendix, containing the Author's Minor Treatises, translated by H. D. Hutton, M.A. [In preparation.

BACON'S ESSAYS with ANNOTATIONS. By R. WHATELY, D.D. late Archbishop of Dublin. New Edition, 8vo. price 10s. 6d.

LORD BACON'S WORKS, collected and edited by J. SPEDDING, M.A. R. L. ELLIS, M.A. and D. D. HEATH. 7 vols. 8vo. price £3. 13s. 6d.

The **SUBJECTION of WOMEN.** By JOHN STUART MILL. New Edition. Post 8vo. 5s.

On **REPRESENTATIVE GOVERNMENT.** By JOHN STUART MILL. Crown 8vo. price 2s.

On **LIBERTY.** By JOHN STUART MILL. New Edition. Post 8vo. 7s. 6d. Crown 8vo. price 1s. 4d.

PRINCIPLES of POLITICAL ECONOMY. By JOHN STUART MILL. Seventh Edition. 2 vols. 8vo. 30s. Or in 1 vol. crown 8vo. price 5s.

ESSAYS on SOME UNSETTLED QUESTIONS of POLITICAL ECONOMY. By JOHN STUART MILL. Second Edition. 8vo. 6s. 6d.

UTILITARIANISM. By JOHN STUART MILL. New Edition. 8vo. 5s

DISSERTATIONS and DISCUSSIONS: Political, Philosophical, and Historical. By JOHN STUART MILL. New Editions. 4 vols. 8vo. price £2. 7s.

EXAMINATION of Sir. W. HAMILTON'S PHILOSOPHY, and of the Principal Philosophical Questions discussed in his Writings. By JOHN STUART MILL. Fourth Edition. 8vo. 16s.

An **OUTLINE of the NECESSARY LAWS of THOUGHT;** a Treatise on Pure and Applied Logic. By the Most Rev. W. THOMSON, Lord Archbishop of York, D.D. F.R.S. New Edition. Crown 8vo. price 6s.

PRINCIPLES of ECONOMICAL PHILOSOPHY. By HENRY DUNNING MACLEOD, M.A. Barrister-at-Law. Second Edition. In Two Volumes. VOL. I. 8vo. price 15s. VOL. II. PART I. price 12s.

A **SYSTEM of LOGIC, RATIOCINATIVE and INDUCTIVE.** By JOHN STUART MILL. Ninth Edition. Two vols. 8vo. 25s.

SPEECHES of the RIGHT HON. LORD MACAULAY, corrected Himself. People's Edition, crown 8vo. 3s. 6d.

The **ORATION of DEMOSTHENES on the CROWN.** Translated by the Right Hon. Sir R. P. COLLIER. Crown 8vo. price 5s.

FAMILIES of SPEECH: Four Lectures delivered before the Royal Institution of Great Britain. By the Rev. F. W. FARRAR, D.D. F.R.S. New Edition. Crown 8vo. 3s. 6d.

CHAPTERS on LANGUAGE. By the Rev. F. W. FARRAR, D.D. F.R.S. New Edition. Crown 8vo. 5s.

HANDBOOK of the ENGLISH LANGUAGE. For the use of Students of the Universities and the Higher Classes in Schools. By R. G. LATHAM, M.A. M.D. &c. late Fellow of King's College, Cambridge ; late Professor of English in Univ. Coll. Lond. The Ninth Edition. Crown 8vo. price 6s.

A **DICTIONARY of the ENGLISH LANGUAGE.** By R. G. LATHAM, M.A. M.D. Founded on the Dictionary of Dr. SAMUEL JOHNSON, as edited by the Rev. H. J. TODD, with numerous Emendations and Additions. In Four Volumes, 4to. price £7.

A **PRACTICAL ENGLISH DICTIONARY,** on the Plan of White's English-Latin and Latin-English Dictionaries. By JOHN T. WHITE, D.D. Oxon. and T. C. DONKIN, M.A. Assistant-Master, King Edward's Grammar School, Birmingham. Post 8vo. [In the press.

THESAURUS of ENGLISH WORDS and PHRASES, classified and arranged so as to facilitate the Expression of Ideas, and assist in Literary Composition. By P. M. ROGET, M.D. New Edition. Crown 8vo. 10s. 6d.

LECTURES on the SCIENCE of LANGUAGE. By F. MAX MÜLLER, M.A. &c. The Eighth Edition. 2 vols. crown 8vo. 16s.

MANUAL of ENGLISH LITERATURE, Historical and Critical. By THOMAS ARNOLD, M.A. New Edition. Crown 8vo. 7s. 6d.

SOUTHEY'S DOCTOR, complete in One Volume. Edited by the Rev. J. W. WARTER, B.D. Square crown 8vo. 12s. 6d.

HISTORICAL and CRITICAL COMMENTARY on the OLD TESTA-MENT; with a New Translation. By M. M. KALISCH. Ph.D. VOL. I. Genesis, 8vo. 18s. or adapted for the General Reader, 12s. VOL. II. Exodus, 15s. or adapted for the General Reader, 12s. VOL. III. Leviticus, PART I. 15s. or adapted for the General Reader, 8s. VOL. IV. Leviticus, PART II. 15s. or adapted for the General Reader, 8s.

A DICTIONARY of ROMAN and GREEK ANTIQUITIES, with about Two Thousand Engravings on Wood from Ancient Originals, illustrative of the Industrial Arts and Social Life of the Greeks and Romans. By A. RICH, B.A. Third Edition, revised and improved. Crown 8vo. price 7s. 6d.

A LATIN-ENGLISH DICTIONARY. By JOHN T. WHITE, D.D. Oxon. and J. E. RIDDLE, M.A. Oxon. Revised Edition. 2 vols. 4to. 42s.

WHITE'S COLLEGE LATIN-ENGLISH DICTIONARY (Intermediate Size), abridged for the use of University Students from the Parent Work (as above). Medium 8vo. 18s.

WHITE'S JUNIOR STUDENT'S COMPLETE LATIN-ENGLISH and ENGLISH-LATIN DICTIONARY. New Edition. Square 12mo. price 12s.

Separately { The ENGLISH-LATIN DICTIONARY, price 5s. 6d.
{ The LATIN-ENGLISH DICTIONARY, price 7s. 6d.

A LATIN-ENGLISH DICTIONARY, adapted for the Use of Middle-Class Schools. By JOHN T. WHITE, D.D. Oxon. Square fcp. 8vo. price 3s.

An ENGLISH-GREEK LEXICON, containing all the Greek Words used by Writers of good authority. By C. D. YONGE, B.A. New Edition. 4to. price 21s.

Mr. YONGE'S NEW LEXICON, English and Greek, abridged from his larger work (as above). Revised Edition. Square 12mo. price 8s. 6d.

A GREEK-ENGLISH LEXICON. Compiled by H. G. LIDDELL, D.D. Dean of Christ Church, and R. SCOTT, D.D. Dean of Rochester. Sixth Edition. Crown 4to. price 36s.

A LEXICON, GREEK and ENGLISH, abridged from LIDDELL and SCOTT's Greek-English Lexicon. Fourteenth Edition. Square 12mo. 7s. 6d.

A PRACTICAL DICTIONARY of the FRENCH and ENGLISH LAN-GUAGES. By L. CONTANSEAU. Revised Edition. Post 8vo. 10s. 6d.

CONTANSEAU'S POCKET DICTIONARY, French and English, abridged from the above by the Author. New Edition. Square 18mo. 3s. 6d.

NEW PRACTICAL DICTIONARY of the GERMAN LANGUAGE; German-English and English-German. By the Rev. W. L. BLACKLEY, M.A. and Dr. CARL MARTIN FRIEDLÄNDER. Post 8vo. 7s. 6d.

The MASTERY of LANGUAGES; or, the Art of Speaking Foreign Tongues Idiomatically. By THOMAS PRENDERGAST. 8vo. 6s.

Miscellaneous Works and *Popular Metaphysics.*

LECTURES delivered in **AMERICA** in **1874.** By CHARLES KINGSLEY, F.L.S. F.G.S. late Rector of Eversley. Crown 8vo. price 5s.

THE MISCELLANEOUS WORKS of **THOMAS ARNOLD, D.D.** Late Head Master of Rugby School and Regius Professor of Modern History in the University of Oxford, collected and republished. 8vo. 7s. 6d.

MISCELLANEOUS and **POSTHUMOUS WORKS** of the **Late HENRY** THOMAS BUCKLE. Edited, with a Biographical Notice, by HELEN TAYLOR. 3 vols. 8vo. price 52s. 6d.

MISCELLANEOUS WRITINGS of **JOHN CONINGTON, M.A.** late Corpus Professor of Latin in the University of Oxford. Edited by J. A. SYMONDS, M.A. With a Memoir by H. J. S. SMITH, M.A. 2 vols. 8vo. 28s.

ESSAYS, CRITICAL and **BIOGRAPHICAL.** Contributed to the *Edinburgh Review.* By HENRY ROGERS. New Edition, with Additions. 2 vols. crown 8vo. price 12s.

ESSAYS on some THEOLOGICAL CONTROVERSIES of the **TIME.** Contributed chiefly to the *Edinburgh Review.* By HENRY ROGERS. New Edition, with Additions. Crown 8vo. price 6s.

RECREATIONS of a **COUNTRY PARSON.** By A. K. H. B. FIRST and SECOND SERIES, crown 8vo. 3s. 6d. each.

The Common-place Philosopher in Town and Country. By A. K. H. B. Crown 8vo. price 3s. 6d.

Leisure Hours in Town; Essays Consolatory, Æsthetical, Moral, Social, and Domestic. By A. K. H. B. Crown 8vo. 3s. 6d.

The Autumn Holidays of a Country Parson; Essays contributed to *Fraser's Magazine,* &c. By A. K. H. B. Crown 8vo. 3s. 6d.

Seaside Musings on Sundays and Week-Days. By A. K. H. B. Crown 8vo. price 3s. 6d.

The Graver Thoughts of a Country Parson. By A. K. H. B. FIRST, SECOND, and THIRD SERIES, crown 8vo. 3s. 6d. each.

Critical Essays of a Country Parson, selected from Essays contributed to *Fraser's Magazine.* By A. K. H. B. Crown 8vo. 3s. 6d.

Sunday Afternoons at the Parish Church of a Scottish University City. By A. K. H. B. Crown 8vo. 3s. 6d.

Lessons of Middle Age; with some Account of various Cities and Men. By A. K. H. B. Crown 8vo. 3s. 6d.

Counsel and Comfort spoken from a City Pulpit. By A. K. H. B. Crown 8vo. price 3s. 6d.

Changed Aspects of Unchanged Truths; Memorials of St. Andrews Sundays. By A. K. H. B. Crown 8vo. 3s. 6d.

Present-day Thoughts; Memorials of St. Andrews Sundays. By A. K. H. B. Crown 8vo. 3s. 6d.

Landscapes, Churches, and Moralities. By A. K. H. B. Crown 8vo. price 3s. 6d.

SHORT STUDIES on GREAT SUBJECTS. By JAMES ANTHONY FROUDE, M.A. late Fellow of Exeter Coll. Oxford. 2 vols. crown 8vo. price 12s.

LORD MACAULAY'S MISCELLANEOUS WRITINGS:—
LIBRARY EDITION. 2 vols. 8vo. Portrait, 21s.
PEOPLE's EDITION. 1 vol. crown 8vo. 4s. 6d.

LORD MACAULAY'S MISCELLANEOUS WRITINGS and SPEECHES.
STUDENT's EDITION, in crown 8vo. price 6s.

The Rev. SYDNEY SMITH'S ESSAYS contributed to the Edinburgh Review. Authorised Edition, complete in 1 vol. Crown 8vo. price 2s. 6d.

The Rev. SYDNEY SMITH'S MISCELLANEOUS WORKS; including his Contributions to the *Edinburgh Review.* Crown 8vo. 6s.

The WIT and WISDOM of the Rev. SYDNEY SMITH; a Selection of the most memorable Passages in his Writings and Conversation. 16mo. 3s. 6d.

The ECLIPSE of FAITH; or, a Visit to a Religious Sceptic. By HENRY ROGERS. Latest Edition. Fcp. 8vo. price 5s.

Defence of the Eclipse of Faith, by its Author; a rejoinder to Dr. Newman's *Reply.* Latest Edition. Fcp 8vo. price 3s. 6d.

CHIPS from a GERMAN WORKSHOP; Essays on the Science of Religion, on Mythology, Traditions, and Customs, and on the Science of Language. By F. MAX MÜLLER, M.A. &c. 4 vols. 8vo. £2. 18s.

ANALYSIS of the PHENOMENA of the HUMAN MIND. By JAMES MILL. A New Edition, with Notes, Illustrative and Critical, by ALEXANDER BAIN, ANDREW FINDLATER, and GEORGE GROTE. Edited, with additional Notes, by JOHN STUART MILL. 2 vols. 8vo. price 28s.

An INTRODUCTION to MENTAL PHILOSOPHY, on the Inductive Method. By J. D. MORELL, M.A. LL.D. 8vo. 12s.

ELEMENTS of PSYCHOLOGY, containing the Analysis of the Intellectual Powers. By J. D. MORELL, M.A. LL.D. Post 8vo. 7s. 6d.

The SECRET of HEGEL; being the Hegelian System in Origin, Principle, Form, and Matter. By J. H. STIRLING, LL.D. 2 vols. 8vo. 28s.

SIR WILLIAM HAMILTON; being the Philosophy of Perception: an Analysis. By J. H. STIRLING, LL.D. 8vo. 5s.

The SENSES and the INTELLECT. By ALEXANDER BAIN, M.D. Professor of Logic in the University of Aberdeen. Third Edition. 8vo. 15s.

The EMOTIONS and the WILL. By ALEXANDER BAIN, LL.D. Professor of Logic in the University of Aberdeen. Third Edition, thoroughly revised, and in great part re-written. 8vo. price 15s.

MENTAL and MORAL SCIENCE: a Compendium of Psychology and Ethics. By the same Author. Third Edition. Crown 8vo. 10s. 6d. Or separately: PART I. *Mental Science,* 6s. 6d. PART II. *Moral Science,* 4s. 6d.

LOGIC, DEDUCTIVE and INDUCTIVE. By the same Author. In Two PARTS, crown 8vo. 10s. 6d. Each Part may be had separately:—
PART I. *Deduction,* 4s. PART II. *Induction,* 6s. 6d.

A BUDGET of PARADOXES. By AUGUSTUS DE MORGAN, F.R.A.S. and C.P.S. 8vo. 15s.

APPARITIONS; a Narrative of Facts. By the Rev. B. W. SAVILE, M.A. Author of 'The Truth of the Bible' &c. Crown 8vo. price 4s. 6d.

A TREATISE of HUMAN NATURE, being an Attempt to Introduce the Experimental Method of Reasoning into Moral Subjects; followed by Dialogues concerning Natural Religion. By DAVID HUME. Edited, with Notes, &c. by T. H. GREEN, Fellow and Tutor, Ball. Coll. and T. H. GROSE, Fellow and Tutor, Queen's Coll. Oxford. 2 vols. 8vo. 28s.

ESSAYS MORAL, POLITICAL, and LITERARY. By DAVID HUME. By the same Editors. 2 vols. 8vo. price 28s.

The PHILOSOPHY of NECESSITY; or, Natural Law as applicable to Mental, Moral, and Social Science. By CHARLES BRAY. 8vo. 9s.

UEBERWEG'S SYSTEM of LOGIC and HISTORY of LOGICAL DOCTRINES. Translated, with Notes and Appendices, by T. M. LINDSAY, M.A. F.R.S.E. 8vo. price 16s.

FRAGMENTARY PAPERS on SCIENCE and other Subjects. By the late Sir H. HOLLAND, Bart. Edited by his Son, the Rev. F. HOLLAND. 8vo. price 14s.

Astronomy, Meteorology, Popular Geography, &c.

BRINKLEY'S ASTRONOMY. Revised and partly re-written, with Additional Chapters, and an Appendix of Questions for Examination. By J. W. STUBBS, D.D. Fellow and Tutor of Trinity College, Dublin, and F. BRUNNOW, Ph.D. Astronomer Royal of Ireland. Crown 8vo. price 6s.

OUTLINES of ASTRONOMY. By Sir J. F. W. HERSCHEL, Bart. M.A. Latest Edition, with Plates and Diagrams. Square crown 8vo. 12s.

ESSAYS on ASTRONOMY, a Series of Papers on Planets and Meteors, the Sun and Sun-surrounding Space, Stars and Star-Cloudlets; with a Dissertation on the approaching Transit of Venus. By RICHARD A. PROCTOR, B.A. With 10 Plates and 24 Woodcuts. 8vo. 12s.

THE TRANSITS of VENUS; a Popular Account of Past and Coming Transits, from the first observed by Horrocks A.D. 1639 to the Transit of A.D. 2012. By R. A. PROCTOR, B.A. Second Edition, with 20 Plates (12 coloured) and 38 Woodcuts. Crown 8vo. 8s. 6d.

The UNIVERSE and the COMING TRANSITS : Presenting Researches into and New Views respecting the Constitution of the Heavens; together with an Investigation of the Conditions of the Coming Transits of Venus. By R. A. PROCTOR, B.A. With 22 Charts and 22 Woodcuts. 8vo. 16s.

The MOON; her Motions, Aspect, Scenery, and Physical Condition. By R. A. PROCTOR, B.A. With Plates, Charts, Woodcuts, and Three Lunar Photographs. Crown 8vo. 15s.

The SUN; RULER, LIGHT, FIRE, and LIFE of the PLANETARY SYSTEM. By R. A. PROCTOR, B.A. Second Edition, with 10 Plates (7 coloured) and 107 Figures on Wood. Crown 8vo. 14s.

OTHER WORLDS THAN OURS; the Plurality of Worlds Studied under the Light of Recent Scientific Researches. By R. A. PROCTOR, B.A. Third Edition, with 14 Illustrations. Crown 8vo. 10s. 6d.

The ORBS AROUND US; Familiar Essays on the Moon and Planets, Meteors and Comets, the Sun and Coloured Pairs of Stars. By R. A. PROCTOR, B.A. Second Edition, with Charts and 4 Diagrams. Crown 8vo. price 7s. 6d.

SATURN and its SYSTEM. By R. A. PROCTOR, B.A. 8vo. with 14 Plates, 14s.

A NEW STAR ATLAS, for the Library, the School, and the Observatory, in Twelve Circular Maps (with Two Index Plates). Intended as a Companion to 'Webb's Celestial Objects for Common Telescopes.' With a Letterpress Introduction on the Study of the Stars, illustrated by 9 Diagrams. . By R. A. PROCTOR, B.A. Crown 8vo. 5s.

SCHELLEN'S SPECTRUM ANALYSIS, in its application to Terrestrial Substances and the Physical Constitution of the Heavenly Bodies. Translated by JANE and C. LASSELL; edited, with Notes, by W. HUGGINS, LL.D. F.R.S. With 13 Plates (6 coloured) and 223 Woodcuts. 8vo. price 28s.

CELESTIAL OBJECTS for COMMON TELESCOPES. By the Rev. T. W. WEBB, M.A. F.R.A.S. Third Edition, revised and enlarged; with Maps, Plate, and Woodcuts. Crown 8vo. price 7s. 6d.

AIR and RAIN; the Beginnings of a Chemical Climatology. By ROBERT ANGUS SMITH, Ph.D. F.R.S. F.C.S. With 8 Illustrations. 8vo. 24s.

AIR and its RELATIONS to LIFE; being, with some Additions, the Substance of a Course of Lectures delivered at the Royal Institution of Great Britain in 1874. By WALTER NOEL HARTLEY, F.C.S. Demonstrator of Chemistry at King's College, London. With 66 Woodcuts. Small 8vo. 6s.

NAUTICAL SURVEYING, an INTRODUCTION to the PRACTICAL and THEORETICAL STUDY of. By J. K. LAUGHTON, M.A. Small 8vo. 6s.

MAGNETISM and DEVIATION of the COMPASS. For the Use of Students in Navigation and Science Schools. By J. MERRIFIELD, LL.D. 18mo. 1s. 6d,

DOVE'S LAW of STORMS, considered in connexion with the Ordinary Movements of the Atmosphere. Translated by R. H. SCOTT, M.A. 8vo. 10s. 6d.

KEITH JOHNSTON'S GENERAL DICTIONARY of GEOGRAPHY, Descriptive, Physical, Statistical, and Historical; forming a complete Gazetteer of the World. New Edition, revised and corrected. 1 vol. 8vo. [Nearly ready.

The PUBLIC SCHOOLS ATLAS of MODERN GEOGRAPHY. In 31 Coloured Maps, exhibiting clearly the more important Physical Features of the Countries delineated, and Noting all the Chief Places of Historical, Commercial, or Social Interest. Edited, with an Introduction, by the Rev. G. BUTLER, M.A. Imperial 8vo. bound, price 5s. or imperial 4to. 5s. cloth.

The PUBLIC SCHOOLS MANUAL of MODERN GEOGRAPHY. By the Rev. GEORGE BUTLER, M.A. Principal of Liverpool College; Editor of 'The Public Schools Atlas of Modern Geography.' [In preparation.

The PUBLIC SCHOOLS ATLAS of ANCIENT GEOGRAPHY Edited, with an Introduction on the Study of Ancient Geography, by the Rev. GEORGE BUTLER, M.A. Principal of Liverpool College. [In preparation.

MAUNDER'S TREASURY of GEOGRAPHY, Physical, Historical, Descriptive, and Political. Edited by W. HUGHES, F.R.G.S. Revised Edition, with 7 Maps and 16 Plates. Fcp. 6s. cloth, or 10s. bound in calf.

Natural History and Popular Science.

TEXT-BOOKS of SCIENCE, MECHANICAL and PHYSICAL, adapted for the use of Artisans and of Students in Public and Science Schools. Edited by T. M. GOODEVE, M.A. and C. W. MERRIFIELD, F.R.S.

Edited by T. M. GOODEVE, M.A.

ANDERSON'S Strength of Materials, small 8vo. 3s. 6d.
BLOXAM'S Metals, 3s. 6d.
GOODEVE'S Elements of Mechanism, 3s. 6d.
———— Principles of Mechanics, 3s. 6d.
GRIFFIN'S Algebra and Trigonometry, 3s. 6d. Notes, 3s.6d.
JENKIN'S Electricity and Magnetism, 3s. 6d.
MAXWELL'S Theory of Heat, 3s. 6d.
MERRIFIELD'S Technical Arithmetic and Mensuration, 3s. 6d. Key, 3s. 6d.
MILLER'S Inorganic Chemistry, 3s. 6d.
SHELLEY'S Workshop Appliances, 3s. 6d.
WATSON'S Plane and Solid Geometry, 3s. 6d.

Edited by C. W. MERRIFIELD, F.R.S.

ARMSTRONG'S Organic Chemistry, 3s. 6d.
THORPE'S Quantitative Chemical Analysis, 4s. 6d.
THORPE & MUIR'S Qualitative Analysis, 3s. 6d.

ELEMENTARY TREATISE on PHYSICS, Experimental and Applied. Translated and edited from GANOT'S Éléments de Physique by E. ATKINSON, Ph.D. F.C.S. Seventh Edition, revised and enlarged; with 4 Coloured Plates and 758 Woodcuts. Post 8vo. 15s.

NATURAL PHILOSOPHY for GENERAL READERS and YOUNG PERSONS; being a Course of Physics divested of Mathematical Formulæ expressed in the language of daily life. Translated from GANOT'S Cours de Physique and by E. ATKINSON, Ph.D. F.C.S. Second Edition, with 2 Plates and 429 Woodcuts. Crown 8vo. price 7s. 6d.

HELMHOLTZ'S POPULAR LECTURES on SCIENTIFIC SUBJECTS. Translated by E. ATKINSON, Ph.D. F.C.S. Professor of Experimental Science, Staff College. With an Introduction by Professor TYNDALL. 8vo. with numerous Woodcuts, price 12s. 6d.

On the SENSATIONS of TONE as a Physiological Basis for the Theory of Music. By HERMANN L. F. HELMHOLTZ, M.D. Professor of Physics in the University of Berlin. Translated, with the Author's sanction, from the Third German Edition, with Additional Notes and an Additional Appendix, by ALEXANDER J. ELLIS, F.R.S. &c. 8vo. price 36s.

The HISTORY of MODERN MUSIC, a Course of Lectures delivered at the Royal Institution of Great Britain. By JOHN HULLAH, Professor of Vocal Music in Queen's College and Bedford College, and Organist of Charterhouse. New Edition, 1 vol. post 8vo. [In the press

SOUND. By JOHN TYNDALL, LL.D. D.C.L. F.R.S. Third Edition, including Recent Researches on Fog-Signalling; Portrait and Woodcuts. Crown 8vo. 10s. 6d.

HEAT a MODE of MOTION. By JOHN TYNDALL, LL.D. D.C.L. F.R.S. Fifth Edition. Plate and Woodcuts. Crown 8vo. 10s. 6d.

CONTRIBUTIONS to MOLECULAR PHYSICS in the DOMAIN of RADIANT HEAT. By J. TYNDALL, LL.D. D.C.L. F.R.S. With 2 Plates and 31 Woodcuts. 8vo. 16s.

RESEARCHES on DIAMAGNETISM and MAGNE-CRYSTALLIC ACTION; including the Question of Diamagnetic Polarity. By J. TYNDALL, M.D. D.C.L. F.R.S. With 6 plates and many Woodcuts. 8vo. 14s.

NOTES of a COURSE of SEVEN LECTURES on ELECTRICAL PHENOMENA and THEORIES, delivered at the Royal Institution, A.D. 1870. By JOHN TYNDALL, LL.D., D.C.L., F.R.S. Crown 8vo. 1s. sewed; 1s. 6d. cloth. ·

SIX LECTURES on LIGHT delivered in America in 1872 and 1873. By JOHN TYNDALL, LL.D. D.C.L. F.R.S. Second Edition, with Portrait, Plate, and 59 Diagrams. Crown 8vo. 7s. 6d.

NOTES of a COURSE of NINE LECTURES on LIGHT delivered at the Royal Institution, A.D. 1869. By JOHN TYNDALL, LL.D. D.C.L. F.R.S. Crown 8vo. price 1s. sewed, or 1s. 6d. cloth.

ADDRESS delivered before the British Association assembled at Belfast. By JOHN TYNDALL, F.R.S. President. 8th Thousand, with New Preface and the Manchester Address. 8vo. 4s. 6d.

FRAGMENTS of SCIENCE. By JOHN TYNDALL, LL.D. D.C.L. F.R.S. New Edition.   [In the press.

LIGHT SCIENCE for LEISURE HOURS; a Series of Familiar Essays on Scientific Subjects, Natural Phenomena, &c. By R. A. PROCTOR, B.A. First and Second Series. Crown 8vo. 7s. 6d. each.

A TREATISE on MAGNETISM, General and Terrestrial. By HUMPHREY LLOYD, D.D. D.C.L., Provost of Trinity College, Dublin. 8vo. 10s. 6d.

ELEMENTARY TREATISE on the WAVE-THEORY of LIGHT. By HUMPHREY LLOYD, D.D. D.C.L. Provost of Trinity College, Dublin. Third Edition, revised and enlarged. 8vo. price 10s. 6d.

The CORRELATION of PHYSICAL FORCES. By the Hon. Sir W. R. GROVE, M.A. F.R.S. one of the Judges of the Court of Common Pleas. Sixth Edition, with other Contributions to Science. 8vo. price 15s.

An ELEMENTARY EXPOSITION of the DOCTRINE of ENERGY. By D. D. HEATH, formerly Fellow of Trinity College, Cambridge. Post 8vo price 4s. 6d.

The COMPARATIVE ANATOMY and PHYSIOLOGY of the VERTE- BRATE ANIMALS. By RICHARD OWEN, F.R.S. D.C.L. With 1,472 Woodcuts. 3 vols. 8vo. £3. 13s. 6d.

PRINCIPLES of ANIMAL MECHANICS. By the Rev. S. HAUGHTON, F.R.S. Fellow of Trin. Coll. Dubl. M.D. Dubl. and D.C.L. Oxon. Second Edition, with 111 Figures on Wood. 8vo. 21s.

ROCKS CLASSIFIED and DESCRIBED. By BERNHARD VON COTTA. English Edition, by P. H. LAWRENCE; with English, German, and French Synonymes. Post 8vo. 14s.

The ANCIENT STONE IMPLEMENTS, WEAPONS, and ORNA- MENTS of GREAT BRITAIN. By JOHN EVANS, F.R.S. F.S.A. With 2 Plates and 476 Woodcuts. 8vo. price 28s.

The NATIVE RACES of the PACIFIC STATES of NORTH AMERICA. By HUBERT HOWE BANCROFT. Vol. I. Wild Tribes, their Manners and Customs, with 6 Maps. 8vo. 25s. Vol. II. Native Races of the Pacific, 25s. Vol. III. Myths and Languages, 25s. To be completed early in the year 1876, in Two more Volumes: Vol. IV. Antiquities and Architectural Remains. Vol. V. Aboriginal History and Migrations; Index to the Entire Work.

PRIMÆVAL WORLD of SWITZERLAND. By Professor OSWALD HEER, of the University of Zurich. Translated by W. S. DALLAS. F.L.S., and edited by JAMES HEYWOOD, M.A., F.R.S. 2 vols. 8vo. with numerous Illustrations. [*In the press.*

The ORIGIN of CIVILISATION and the PRIMITIVE CONDITION of MAN ; Mental and Social Condition of Savages. By Sir JOHN LUBBOCK, Bart. M.P. F.R.S. Third Edition, with 25 Woodcuts. 8vo. 18s.

BIBLE ANIMALS; being a Description of every Living Creature mentioned in the Scriptures, from the Ape to the Coral. By the Rev. J. G. WOOD, M.A. F.L.S. With about 100 Vignettes on Wood. 8vo. 21s.

HOMES WITHOUT HANDS; a Description of the Habitations of Animals, classed according to their Principle of Construction. By the Rev. J. G. WOOD, M.A. F.L.S. With about 140 Vignettes on Wood. 8vo. 14s.

INSECTS AT HOME; a Popular Account of British Insects, their Structure, Habits, and Transformations. By the Rev. J. G. WOOD, M.A. F.L.S. With upwards of 700 Illustrations. 8vo. price 21s.

INSECTS ABROAD; a Popular Account of Foreign Insects, their Structure, Habits, and Transformations. By J. G. WOOD, M.A. F.L.S. Printed and illustrated uniformly with ' Insects at Home.' 8vo. price 21s.

STRANGE DWELLINGS; a description of the Habitations of Animals, abridged from ' Homes without Hands.' By the Rev. J. G. WOOD, M.A. F.L.S. With about 60 Woodcut Illustrations. Crown 8vo. price 7s. 6d.

OUT of DOORS; a Selection of original Articles on Practical Natural History. By the Rev. J. G. WOOD, M.A. F.L.S. With Eleven Illustrations from Original Designs engraved on Wood by G. Pearson. Crown 8vo. price 7s. 6d.

GAME PRESERVERS and BIRD PRESERVERS, or ' Which are our Friends?' By GEORGE FRANCIS MORANT, late Captain 12th Royal Lancers & Major Cape Mounted Riflemen. Crown 8vo. price 5s.

A FAMILIAR HISTORY of BIRDS. By E. STANLEY, D.D. F.R.S. late Lord Bishop of Norwich. Seventh Edition, with Woodcuts. Fcp. 3s. 6d.

The SEA and its LIVING WONDERS. By Dr. GEORGE HARTWIG. Latest revised Edition. 8vo. with many Illustrations, 10s. 6d.

The TROPICAL WORLD. By Dr. GEORGE HARTWIG. With above 160 Illustrations. Latest revised Edition. 8vo. price 10s. 6d.

The SUBTERRANEAN WORLD. By Dr. GEORGE HARTWIG. With 3 Maps and about 80 Woodcuts, including 8 full size of page. 8vo. price 10s. 6d.

The POLAR WORLD, a Popular Description of Man and Nature in the Arctic and Antarctic Regions of the Globe. By Dr. GEORGE HARTWIG. With 8 Chromoxylographs, 3 Maps, and 85 Woodcuts. 8vo. 10s. 6d.

THE AERIAL WORLD. By Dr. G. HARTWIG. New Edition, with 8 Chromoxylographs and 60 Woodcut Illustrations. 8vo. price 21s.

KIRBY and SPENCE'S INTRODUCTION to ENTOMOLOGY, or Elements of the Natural History of Insects. 7th Edition. Crown 8vo. 5s.

MAUNDER'S TREASURY of NATURAL HISTORY, or Popular Dictionary of Birds, Beasts, Fishes, Reptiles, Insects, and Creeping Things. With above 900 Woodcuts. Fcp. 8vo. price 6s. cloth, or 10s. bound in calf.

MAUNDER'S SCIENTIFIC and LITERARY TREASURY. New Edition, thoroughly revised and in great part rewritten, with above 1,000 new Articles, by J. Y. JOHNSON. Fcp. 8vo. 6s. cloth, or 10s. calf.

HANDBOOK of HARDY TREES, SHRUBS, and HERBACEOUS
PLANTS, containing Descriptions, Native Countries, &c. of a Selection of the
Best Species in Cultivation; togethér with Cultural Details, Comparative
Hardiness, Suitability for Particular Positions, &c. By W. B. HEMSLEY. Based on
DECAISNE and NAUDIN's *Manuel de l'Amateur des Jardins*, and including the 264
Original Woodcuts. Medium 8vo. 21s.

A GENERAL SYSTEM of BOTANY DESCRIPTIVE and ANALYTICAL.
I. Outlines of Organography, Anatomy, and Physiology; II. Descriptions and
Illustrations of the Orders. By E. LE MAOUT, and J. DECAISNE, Members of
the Institute of France. Translated by Mrs. HOOKER. The Orders arranged
after the Method followed in the Universities and Schools of Great Britain, its
Colonies, America, and India; with an Appendix on the Natural Method, and
other Additions, by J. D. HOOKER, F.R.S. &c. Director of the Royal Botanical
Gardens, Kew. With 5,500 Woodcuts. Imperial 8vo. price 52s. 6d.

The TREASURY of BOTANY, or Popular Dictionary of the Vegetable
Kingdom; including a Glossary of Botanical Terms. Edited by J. LINDLEY,
F.R.S. and T. MOORE, F.L.S. assisted by eminent Contributors. With 274
Woodcuts and 20 Steel Plates. Two Parts, fcp. 8vo. 12s. cloth, or 20s. calf.

The ELEMENTS of BOTANY for FAMILIES and SCHOOLS.
Tenth Edition, revised by THOMAS MOORE, F.L.S. Fcp. 8vo. with 154 Woodcuts, 2s. 6d.

The ROSE AMATEUR'S GUIDE. By THOMAS RIVERS. Fourteenth
Edition. Fcp. 8vo. 4s.

LOUDON'S ENCYCLOPÆDIA of PLANTS; comprising the Specific
Character, Description, Culture, History, &c. of all the Plants found in
Great Britain. With upwards of 12,000 Woodcuts. 8vo. 42s.

BRANDE'S DICTIONARY of SCIENCE, LITERATURE, and ART.
Re-edited by the Rev. GEORGE W. COX, M.A. late Scholar of Trinity College,
Oxford; assisted by Contributors of eminent Scientific and Literary Acquire-
ments. New Edition, revised. 3 vols. medium 8vo. 63s.

Chemistry and *Physiology.*

A DICTIONARY of CHEMISTRY and the Allied Branches of other
Sciences. By HENRY WATTS, F.R.S. assisted by eminent Contributors.
Seven Volumes, medium 8vo. price £10, 16s. 6d.

ELEMENTS of CHEMISTRY, Theoretical and Practical. By W. ALLEN
MILLER, M.D. late Prof. of Chemistry, King's Coll. London. New
Edition. 3 vols. 8vo. £3. PART I. CHEMICAL PHYSICS, 15s. PART II.
INORGANIC CHEMISTRY, 21s. PART III. ORGANIC CHEMISTRY, New Edition
in the press.

SELECT METHODS in CHEMICAL ANALYSIS, chiefly INOR-
GANIC. By WILLIAM CROOKES, F.R.S. With 22 Woodcuts. Crown 8vo.
price 12s. 6d.

A PRACTICAL HANDBOOK of DYEING and CALICO PRINTING.
By WILLIAM CROOKES, F.R.S. With 11 Page Plates, 49 Specimens of Dyed and
Printed Fabrics, and 36 Woodcuts. 8vo. 42s.

OUTLINES of PHYSIOLOGY, Human and Comparative. By JOHN
MARSHALL, F.R.C.S. Surgeon to the University College Hospital. 2 vols.
crown 8vo. with 122 Woodcuts, 32*s.*

PHYSIOLOGICAL ANATOMY and PHYSIOLOGY of MAN. By the
late R. B. TODD, M.D. F.R.S. and W. BOWMAN, F.R.S. of King's College.
With numerous Illustrations. Vol. II. 8vo. 25*s.*

> VOL. I. New Edition by Dr. LIONEL S. BEALE, F.R.S. in course of publi-
> cation, with many Illustrations. PARTS I. and II. price 7*s.* 6*d.* each.

HEALTH in the HOUSE; a Series of Lectures on Elementary Physiology in its application to the Daily Wants of Man and Animals, delivered to
the Wives and Children of Working Men in Leeds and Saltaire. By CATHERINE
M. BUCKTON. Third Edition, revised. Small 8vo. Woodcuts, 5*s.*

The Fine Arts, and *Illustrated Editions.*

A DICTIONARY of ARTISTS of the ENGLISH SCHOOL: Painters,
Sculptors, Architects, Engravers, and Ornamentists; with Notices of their Lives
and Works. By S. REDGRAVE. 8vo. 16*s.*

POEMS. By WILLIAM B. SCOTT. I. Ballads and Tales. II. Studies
from Nature. III. Sonnets &c. Illustrated by 17 Etchings by W. B. SCOTT
(the Author) and L. ALMA TADEMA. Crown 8vo. price 15*s.*

HALF-HOUR LECTURES on the HISTORY and PRACTICE of the
FINE and ORNAMENTAL ARTS. By W. B. SCOTT, Assistant Inspector in
Art, Department of Science and Art. Third Edition, with 50 Woodcuts. Crown
8vo. 8*s.* 6*d.*

The THREE CATHEDRALS DEDICATED to ST. PAUL, in LONDON;
their History from the Foundation of the First Building in the Sixth Century
to the Proposals for the Adornment of the Present Cathedral. By WILLIAM
LONGMAN, F.A.S. With numerous Illustrations. Square crown 8vo. 21*s.*

IN FAIRYLAND; Pictures from the Elf-World. By RICHARD
DOYLE. With a Poem by W. ALLINGHAM. With Sixteen Plates, containing
Thirty-six Designs printed in Colours. Second Edition. Folio, price 15*s.*

The NEW TESTAMENT, illustrated with Wood Engravings after the
Early Masters, chiefly of the Italian School. Crown 4to. 63*s.* cloth, gilt top;
or £5 5*s.* elegantly bound in morocco.

SACRED and LEGENDARY ART. By MRS. JAMESON.

Legends of the Saints and Martyrs. New Edition, with 19
Etchings and 187 Woodcuts. 2 vols. square crown 8vo. 31*s.* 6*d.*

Legends of the Monastic Orders. New Edition, with 11 Etchings
and 88 Woodcuts. 1 vol. square crown 8vo. 21*s.*

Legends of the Madonna. New Edition, with 27 Etchings and
165 Woodcuts. 1 vol. square crown 8vo. 21*s.*

The History of Our Lord, with that of his Types and Precursors.
Completed by Lady EASTLAKE. Revised Edition, with 31 Etchings and
281 Woodcuts. 2 vols. square crown 8vo. 42*s.*

B

The Useful Arts, Manufactures, &c.

GWILT'S ENCYCLOPÆDIA of ARCHITECTURE, with above 1,600 Engravings on Wood. New Edition, revised and enlarged by WYATT PAPWORTH. 8vo. 52s. 6d.

HINTS on HOUSEHOLD TASTE in FURNITURE, UPHOLSTERY, and other Details. By CHARLES L. EASTLAKE, Architect. New Edition, with about 90 Illustrations. Square crown 8vo. 14s.

PRINCIPLES of MECHANISM, designed for the Use of Students in the Universities, and for Engineering Students generally. By R. WILLIS, M.A. F.R.S. &c. Jacksonian Professor in the University of Cambridge. Second Edition, enlarged; with 374 Woodcuts. 8vo. 18s.

LATHES and TURNING, Simple, Mechanical, and Ornamental. By W. HENRY NORTHCOTT. With about 240 Illustrations. 8vo. 18s.

PERSPECTIVE; or, the Art of Drawing what One Sees. Explained and adapted to the use of those Sketching from Nature. By Lieut. W. H. COLLINS, R.E. F.R.A.S. With 37 Woodcuts. Crown 8vo. price 5s.

INDUSTRIAL CHEMISTRY; a Manual for Manufacturers and for use in Colleges or Technical Schools. Being a Translation of Professors Stohmann and Engler's German Edition of PAYEN'S *Précis de Chimie Industrielle*, by Dr. J. D. BARRY. Edited and supplemented by B. H. PAUL, Ph.D. 8vo. with Plates and Woodcuts.   [*In the press.*

URE'S DICTIONARY of ARTS, MANUFACTURES, and MINES. Seventh Edition, rewritten and enlarged by ROBERT HUNT, F.R.S. assisted by numerous Contributors eminent in Science and the Arts, and familiar with Manufactures. With above 2,100 Woodcuts. 3 vols. medium 8vo. £5 5s.

HANDBOOK of PRACTICAL TELEGRAPHY. By R. S. CULLEY Memb. Inst. C.E. Engineer-in-Chief of Telegraphs to the Post Office. Sixth Edition, with 144 Woodcuts and 5 Plates. 8vo. price 16s.

The ENGINEER'S HANDBOOK; explaining the Principles which should guide the Young Engineer in the Construction of Machinery, with the necessary Rules, Proportions, and Tables By C. S. LOWNDES. Post 8vo. 5s.

ENCYCLOPÆDIA of CIVIL ENGINEERING, Historical, Theoretical, and Practical. By E. CRESY, C.E. With above 3,000 Woodcuts. 8vo. 42s.

OCCASIONAL PAPERS on SUBJECTS connected with CIVIL ENGINEERING, GUNNERY, and Naval Architecture. By MICHAEL SCOTT, Memb. Inst. C.E. & of Inst. N.A. 2 vols. 8vo. with Plates, 42s.

TREATISE on MILLS and MILLWORK. By Sir W. FAIRBAIRN, Bart. F.R.S. New Edition, with 18 Plates and 322 Woodcuts, 2 vols. 8vo. 32s.

USEFUL INFORMATION for ENGINEERS. By Sir W. FAIRBAIRN, Bart. F.R.S. Revised Edition, with Illustrations. 3 vols. crown 8vo. price 31s. 6d.

The APPLICATION of CAST and WROUGHT IRON to Building Purposes. By Sir W. FAIRBAIRN, Bart. F.R.S. Fourth Edition, enlarged; with 6 Plates and 118 Woodcuts. 8vo. price 16s.

A TREATISE on the STEAM ENGINE, in its various Applications to Mines, Mills, Steam Navigation, Railways, and Agriculture. By J. BOURNE, C.E. Eighth Edition; with Portrait, 37 Plates, and 546 Woodcuts. 4to. 42s.

CATECHISM of the STEAM ENGINE, in its various Applications to Mines, Mills, Steam Navigation, Railways, and Agriculture. By the same Author. With 89 Woodcuts. Fcp. 8vo. 6s.

HANDBOOK of the STEAM ENGINE. By the same Author, forming a KEY to the Catechism of the Steam Engine, with 67 Woodcuts. Fcp. 9s.

BOURNE'S RECENT IMPROVEMENTS in the STEAM ENGINE in its various applications to Mines, Mills, Steam Navigation, Railways, and Agriculture. By JOHN BOURNE, C.E. New Edition, with 124 Woodcuts. Fcp. 8vo. 6s.

PRACTICAL TREATISE on METALLURGY, adapted from the last German Edition of Professor KERL'S *Metallurgy* by W. CROOKES, F.R.S. &c. and E. BÖHRIG, Ph.D. M.E. With 625 Woodcuts. 3 vols. 8vo. price £4 19s.

MITCHELL'S MANUAL of PRACTICAL ASSAYING. Fourth Edition, for the most part rewritten, with all the recent Discoveries incorporated, by W. CROOKES, F.R.S. With 199 Woodcuts. 8vo. 31s. 6d.

LOUDON'S ENCYCLOPÆDIA of AGRICULTURE: comprising the Laying-out, Improvement, and Management of Landed Property, and the Cultivation and Economy of Agricultural Produce. With 1,100 Woodcuts. 8vo. 21s.

Loudon's Encyclopædia of Gardening: comprising the Theory and Practice of Horticulture, Floriculture, Arboriculture, and Landscape Gardening. With 1,000 Woodcuts. 8vo. 21s.

Religious and *Moral Works.*

CHRISTIAN LIFE, its COURSE, its HINDRANCES, and its HELPS; Sermons preached mostly in the Chapel of Rugby School. By the late Rev. THOMAS ARNOLD, D.D. 8vo. 7s. 6d.

CHRISTIAN LIFE, its HOPES, its FEARS, and its CLOSE; Sermons preached mostly in the Chapel of Rugby School. By the late Rev. THOMAS ARNOLD, D.D. 8vo. 7s. 6d.

SERMONS chiefly on the INTERPRETATION of SCRIPTURE. By the late Rev. THOMAS ARNOLD, D.D. 8vo. price 7s. 6d.

SERMONS preached in the Chapel of Rugby School; with an Address before Confirmation. By the late Rev. THOMAS ARNOLD, D.D. Fcp. 8vo. 3s. 6d.

THREE ESSAYS on RELIGION: Nature; the Utility of Religion; Theism. By JOHN STUART MILL. 8vo. price 10s. 6d.

INTRODUCTION to the SCIENCE of RELIGION. Four Lecture delivered at the Royal Institution; with Two Essays on False Analogies an the Philosophy of Mythology. By F. MAX MÜLLER, M.A. Crown 8vo. 10s. 6d.

SUPERNATURAL RELIGION; an Inquiry into the Reality of Divine
Revelation. Fifth Edition, carefully revised, with Eighty Pages of New Preface.
2 vols. 8vo. 24s.

ESSAYS on the HISTORY of the CHRISTIAN RELIGION. By JOHN
Earl RUSSELL, K.G. Cabinet Edition, revised. Fcp. 8vo. price 3s. 6d.

The NEW BIBLE COMMENTARY, by Bishops and other Clergy
of the Anglican Church, critically examined by the Right Rev. J. W. COLENSO,
D.D. Bishop of Natal. 8vo. price 25s.

REASONS of FAITH; or, the ORDER of the Christian Argument
Developed and Explained. By the Rev. G. S. DREW, M.A. Second Edition,
revised and enlarged. Fcp. 8vo. price 6s.

The PRIMITIVE and CATHOLIC FAITH in Relation to the Church
of England. By the Rev. B. W. SAVILE, M.A. Rector of Shillingford, Exeter ;
Author of 'Truth of the Bible' &c. 8vo. price 7s.

SYNONYMS of the OLD TESTAMENT, their BEARING on CHRIS-
TIAN FAITH and PRACTICE. By the Rev. R. B. GIRDLESTONE, M.A. 8vo. 15s.

An INTRODUCTION to the THEOLOGY of the CHURCH of
ENGLAND, in an Exposition of the Thirty-nine Articles. By the Rev. T. P.
BOULTBEE, LL.D. New Edition, Fcp. 8vo. price 6s.

An EXPOSITION of the 39 ARTICLES, Historical and Doctrinal.
By E. HAROLD BROWNE, D.D. Lord Bishop of Winchester. New Edit. 8vo. 16s.

The LIFE and EPISTLES of ST. PAUL. By the Rev. W. J.
CONYBEARE, M.A., and the Very Rev. J. S. HOWSON, D.D. Dean of Chester :—
    LIBRARY EDITION, with all the Original Illustrations, Maps, Landscapes on
    Steel, Woodcuts, &c. 2 vols. 4to. 42s.
    INTERMEDIATE EDITION, with a Selection of Maps, Plates, and Woodcuts.
    2 vols. square crown 8vo. 21s.
    STUDENT'S EDITION, revised and condensed, with 46 Illustrations and Maps.
    1 vol. crown 8vo. price 9s.

COMMENTARY on the EPISTLE to the ROMANS. By the Rev.
W. A. O'CONOR, B.A. Crown 8vo. price 3s. 6d.

The EPISTLE to the HEBREWS; with Analytical Introduction and
Notes. By the Rev. W. A. O'CONOR, B.A. Crown 8vo. price 4s. 6d.

A CRITICAL and GRAMMATICAL COMMENTARY on ST. PAUL'S
Epistles. By C. J. ELLICOTT, D.D. Lord Bishop of Gloucester and Bristol. 8vo.

Galatians, Fourth Edition, 8s. 6d.

Ephesians, Fourth Edition, 8s. 6d.

Pastoral Epistles, Fourth Edition, 10s. 6d.

Philippians, Colossians, and Philemon, Third Edition, 10s. 6d.

Thessalonians, Third Edition, 7s. 6d.

HISTORICAL LECTURES on the **LIFE** of **OUR LORD.** By C. J. ELLICOTT, D.D. Bishop of Gloucester and Bristol. Fifth Edition. 8vo. 12s.

EVIDENCE of the **TRUTH** of the **CHRISTIAN RELIGION** derived from the Literal Fulfilment of Prophecy. By ALEXANDER KEITH, D.D. 37th Edition, with Plates, in square 8vo. 12s. 6d.; 39th Edition, in post 8vo. 6s.

HISTORY of ISRAEL. By H. EWALD, late Professor of the Univ. of Göttingen. Translated by J. E. CARPENTER, M.A., with a Preface by RUSSELL MARTINEAU, M.A. 5 vols. 8vo. 63s.

The **ANTIQUITIES of ISRAEL.** By HEINRICH EWALD, late Professor of the University of Göttingen. Translated from the German by HENRY SHAEN SOLLY, M.A. 8vo. price 12s. 6d. *[Nearly ready.*

The **TREASURY of BIBLE KNOWLEDGE**; being a Dictionary of the Books, Persons, Places, Events, and other matters of which mention is made in Holy Scripture. By Rev. J. AYRE, M.A. With Maps, 16 Plates, and numerous Woodcuts. Fcp. 8vo. price 6s. cloth, or 10s. neatly bound in calf.

LECTURES on the **PENTATEUCH** and the **MOABITE STONE.** By the Right Rev. J. W. COLENSO, D.D. Bishop of Natal. 8vo. 12s.

The **PENTATEUCH** and **BOOK** of **JOSHUA CRITICALLY EXAMINED.** By the Right Rev. J. W. COLENSO, D.D. Bishop of Natal. Crown 8vo. 6s.

SOME QUESTIONS of the **DAY.** By the Author of 'Amy Herbert.' Crown 8vo. price 2s. 6d.

THOUGHTS for the **AGE.** By the Author of 'Amy Herbert,' &c. New Edition, revised. Fcp. 8vo, price 3s. 6d.

PASSING THOUGHTS on **RELIGION.** By the Author of 'Amy Herbert.' New Edition. Fcp. 8vo. price 3s. 6d.

The **DOCTRINE** and **PRACTICE** of **CONFESSION** in the **CHURCH** of ENGLAND. By the Rev. W. E. JELF, B.D. sometime Censor of Ch. Ch.; Author of 'Quousque' &c. 8vo. price 7s. 6d.

FASTING COMMUNION, how Binding in England by the Canons. With the Testimony of the Early Fathers. An Historical Essay. By the Rev. H. T. KINGDON, M.A. Second Edition. 8vo. 10s. 6d.

PREPARATION for the **HOLY COMMUNION**; the Devotions chiefly from the Works of JEREMY TAYLOR. By Miss SEWELL. 32mo. 3s.

LYRA GERMANICA, Hymns translated from the German by Miss C. WINKWORTH. Fcp. 8vo. price 5s.

SPIRITUAL SONGS for the **SUNDAYS** and **HOLIDAYS** throughout the Year. By J. S. B. MONSELL, LL.D. Ninth Thousand. Fcp. 8vo. 5s. 18mo. 2s.

ENDEAVOURS after the **CHRISTIAN LIFE**: Discourses. By the Rev. J. MARTINEAU, LL.D. Fifth Edition, carefully revised. Crown 8vo. 7s. 6d.

HYMNS of **PRAISE** and **PRAYER**, collected and edited by the Rev. J. MARTINEAU, LL.D. Crown 8vo. 4s. 6d. 32mo. 1s. 6d.

The **TYPES of GENESIS**, briefly considered as revealing the Development of Human Nature. By ANDREW JUKES. Third Edition. Crown 8vo. 7s. 6d.

The **SECOND DEATH** and the **RESTITUTION of ALL THINGS**; with some Preliminary Remarks on the Nature and Inspiration of Holy Scripture. (A Letter to a Friend.) By ANDREW JUKES. Fourth Edition. Crown 8vo. 3s. 6d.

WHATELY'S INTRODUCTORY LESSONS on the CHRISTIAN
Evidences. 18mo. 6d.

BISHOP JEREMY TAYLOR'S ENTIRE WORKS. With Life by
BISHOP HEBER. Revised and corrected by the Rev. C. P. EDEN. Complete in
Ten Volumes, 8vo. cloth, price £5. 5s.

Travels, Voyages, &c.

The **INDIAN ALPS, and How we Crossed them**: being a Narrative
of Two Years' Residence in the Eastern Himalayas, and Two Months' Tour
into the Interior, towards Kinchinjunga and Mount Everest. By a Lady
PIONEER. With Illustrations from Original Drawings made on the spot by the
Authoress. Imperial 8vo.   [Nearly ready.

TYROL and the TYROLESE; being an Account of the People and
the Land, in their Social, Sporting, and Mountaineering Aspects. By W. A.
BAILLIE GROHMAN. With numerous Illustrations from Sketches by the Author.
Crown 8vo.   [Now ready.

'**The FROSTY CAUCASUS**;' An Account of a Walk through Part of
the Range, and of an Ascent of Elbruz in the Summer of 1874. By F. C. GROVE.
With Eight Illustrations engraved on Wood by E. Whymper, from Photographs
taken during the Journey, and a Map. Crown 8vo. price 15s.

A JOURNEY of 1,000 MILES through EGYPT and NUBIA to the
SECOND CATARACT of the NILE. Being a Personal Narrative of Four and
a Half Months' Life in a Dahabeeyah on the Nile; with some Account of the
Discovery and Excavation of a Rock-cut Chamber, Descriptions of the River,
the Ruins, and the Desert, the People met, the Places visited, the ways and
manners of the Natives, &c. By AMELIA B. EDWARDS. With numerous Illustrations from Drawings by the Authoress, Map, Plans, Facsimiles, &c. Imperial
8vo.   [Nearly ready.

ITALIAN ALPS; Sketches in the Mountains of Ticino, Lombardy,
the Trentino, and Venetia. By DOUGLAS W. FRESHFIELD, Editor of 'The
Alpine Journal.' Square crown 8vo. with Maps and Illustrations, price 15s.

HERE and THERE in the ALPS. By the Hon. FREDERICA PLUNKET.
With Vignette Title. Post 8vo. 6s. 6d.

REMINISCENCES of FEN and MERE. By J. M. HEATHCOTE.
With Maps and numerous Illustrations from Sketches by the Author. 1 vol.
8vo.   [Nearly ready.

TWO YEARS IN FIJI, a Descriptive Narrative of a Residence in the
Fijian Group of Islands; with some Account of the Fortunes of Foreign
Settlers and Colonists up to the Time of the British Annexation. By LITTON
FORBES, M.D. L.R.C.P. F.R.G.S. late Medical Officer to the German Consulate,
Apia, Navigator Islands. Crown 8vo. 8s. 6d.

EIGHT YEARS in CEYLON. By Sir SAMUEL W. BAKER, M.A.
F.R.G.S. New Edition, with Illustrations engraved on Wood, by G. Pearson.
Crown 8vo. 7s. 6d.

The RIFLE and the HOUND in CEYLON. By Sir SAMUEL W.
BAKER, M.A. F.R.G.S. New Edition, with Illustrations engraved on Wood by
G. Pearson. Crown 8vo. 7s. 6d.

MEETING the SUN; a Journey all round the World through Egypt,
China, Japan, and California. By WILLIAM SIMPSON, F.R.G.S. With 48 Helio-
types and Wood Engravings from Drawings by the Author. Medium 8vo. 24s.

UNTRODDEN PEAKS and UNFREQUENTED VALLEYS; a Mid-summer Ramble among the Dolomites. By AMELIA B. EDWARDS. With a Map and 27 Wood Engravings. Medium 8vo. 21s.

The DOLOMITE MOUNTAINS; Excursions through Tyrol, Carinthia, Carniola, and Friuli, 1861-1863. By J. GILBERT and G. C. CHURCHILL, F.R.G.S. With numerous Illustrations. Square crown 8vo. 21s.

The VALLEYS of TIROL; their Traditions and Customs, and how to Visit them. By Miss R. H. BUSK, Author of 'The Folk-Lore of Rome,' &c. With Maps and Frontispiece. Crown 8vo. 12s. 6d.

The ALPINE CLUB MAP of SWITZERLAND, with parts of the Neighbouring Countries, on the Scale of Four Miles to an Inch. Edited by R. C. NICHOLS, F.S.A. F.R.G.S. In Four Sheets, price 42s. or mounted in a case, 52s. 6d. Each Sheet may be had separately, price 12s. or mounted in a case, 15s.

MAP of the CHAIN of MONT BLANC, from an Actual Survey in 1863-1864. By ADAMS-REILLY, F.R.G.S. M.A.C. Published under the Authority of the Alpine Club. In Chromolithography on extra stout drawing-paper 28in. × 17in. price 10s. or mounted on canvas in a folding case, 12s. 6d.

HOW to SEE NORWAY. By Captain J. R. CAMPBELL. With Map and 5 Woodcuts. Fcp. 8vo. price 5s.

GUIDE to the PYRENEES, for the use of Mountaineers. By CHARLES PACKE. With Map and Illustrations. Crown 8vo. 7s. 6d.

The ALPINE GUIDE. By JOHN BALL, M.R.I.A. late President of the Alpine Club. 3 vols. post 8vo. Thoroughly Revised Editions, with Maps and Illustrations:—I. *Western Alps*, 6s. 6d. II. *Central Alps*, 7s. 6d. III. *Eastern Alps*, 10s. 6d. Or in Ten Parts, price 2s. 6d. each.

Introduction on Alpine Travelling in General, and on the Geology of the Alps, price 1s. Each of the Three Volumes or Parts of the *Alpine Guide* may be had with this INTRODUCTION prefixed, price 1s. extra.

VISITS to REMARKABLE PLACES: Old Halls, Battle-Fields, and Scenes Illustrative of Striking Passages in English History and Poetry. By WILLIAM HOWITT. 2 vols. square crown 8vo. with Woodcuts, 25s.

Works of Fiction.

HIGGLEDY-PIGGLEDY; or, Stories for Everybody and Everybody's Children. By the Right Hon. E. M. KNATCHBULL-HUGESSEN, M.P. With Nine Illustrations from Original Designs by R. Doyle, engraved on Wood by G. Pearson. Crown 8vo. price 6s.

WHISPERS from FAIRYLAND. By the Right Hon. E. H. KNATCH-BULL-HUGESSEN, M.P. With Nine Illustrations from Original Designs engraved on Wood by G. Pearson. Crown 8vo. price 6s.

LADY WILLOUGHBY'S DIARY, 1635—1663; Charles the First, the Protectorate, and the Restoration. Reproduced in the Style of the Period to which the Diary relates. Crown 8vo. price 7s. 6d.

TALES of the TEUTONIC LANDS. By the Rev. G. W. Cox, M.A. and E. H. JONES. Crown 8vo. 10s. 6d.

The FOLK-LORE of ROME, collected by Word of Mouth from the People. By Miss R. H. BUSK, Author of ' Patrañas,' &c. Crown 8vo. 12s. 6d.

NOVELS and TALES. By the Right Hon. B. DISRAELI, M.P.
Cabinet Edition, complete in Ten Volumes, crown 8vo. price £3.

LOTHAIR, 6s.	HENRIETTA TEMPLE, 6s.
CONINGSBY, 6s.	CONTARINI FLEMING, &c. 6s.
SYBIL, 6s.	ALROY, IXION, &c. 6s.
TANCRED, 6s.	The YOUNG DUKE, &c. 6s.
VENETIA, 6s.	VIVIAN GREY ,6s.

The **MODERN NOVELIST'S LIBRARY.** Each Work in crown 8vo.
complete in a Single Volume :—

ATHERSTONE PRIORY, 2s. boards ; 2s. 6d. cloth.
MADEMOISELLE MORI, 2s. boards ; 2s. 6d. cloth.
MELVILLE'S GLADIATORS, 2s boards ; 2s. 6d. cloth.
———— GOOD FOR NOTHING, 2s. boards ; 2s. 6d. cloth.
———— HOLMBY HOUSE, 2s. boards ; 2s. 6d. cloth.
———— INTERPRETER, 2s. boards ; 2s. 6d. cloth.
———— KATE COVENTRY, 2s. boards ; 2s. 6d. cloth.
———— QUEEN'S MARIES, 2s. boards ; 2s. 6d. cloth.
———— DIGBY GRAND, 2s. boards ; 2s. 6d. cloth.
———— GENERAL BOUNCE, 2s. boards ; 2s. 6d. cloth.
TROLLOPE'S WARDEN, 1s. 6d. boards ; 2s. cloth.
————————BARCHESTER TOWERS, 2s. boards ; 2s. 6d. cloth.
BRAMLEY-MOORE'S SIX SISTERS of the VALLEYS, 2s. boards ; 2s. 6d. cloth.
The BURGOMASTER'S FAMILY, 2s. boards ; 2s. 6d. cloth.

CABINET EDITION of STORIES and TALES by Miss SEWELL:—

AMY HERBERT, 2s. 6d.	IVORS, 2s. 6d.
GERTRUDE, 2s. 6d.	KATHARINE ASHTON, 2s. 6d.
The EARL'S DAUGHTER, 2s. 6d.	MARGARET PERCIVAL, 3s. 6d.
EXPERIENCE of LIFE, 2s. 6d.	LANETON PARSONAGE, 3s. 6d.
CLEVE HALL, 2s. 6d.	URSULA, 3s. 6d.

BECKER'S GALLUS; or, Roman Scenes of the Time of Augustus :
with Notes and Excursuses. New Edition. Post 8vo. 7s. 6d.

BECKER'S CHARICLES: a Tale illustrative of Private Life among the
Ancient Greeks : with Notes and Excursuses. New Edition. Post 8vo. 7s. 6d.

Poetry and *The Drama.*

POEMS. By WILLIAM B. SCOTT. I. Ballads and Tales. II. Studies
from Nature. III. Sonnets &c. Illustrated by 17 Etchings by L. ALMA
TADEMA and WILLIAM B. SCOTT. Crown 8vo. price 15s.

MOORE'S IRISH MELODIES, Maclise's Edition, with 161 Steel Plates
from Original Drawings. Super-royal 8vo. 31s. 6d.

Miniature Edition of Moore's Irish Melodies, with Maclise's Designs (as above) reduced in Lithography. Imp. 16mo. 10s. 6d.

BALLADS and LYRICS of OLD FRANCE; with other Poems. By
A. LANG, Fellow of Merton College, Oxford. Square fcp. 8vo. price 5s.

MOORE'S LALLA ROOKH. Tenniel's Edition, with 68 Wood
Engravings from Original Drawings and other Illustrations. Fcp. 4to. 21s.

SOUTHEY'S POETICAL WORKS, with the Author's last Corrections and copyright Additions. Medium 8vo. with Portrait and Vignette, 14s.

LAYS of ANCIENT ROME; with **IVRY** and the **ARMADA**. By the Right Hon. Lord MACAULAY. 16mo. 3s. 6d.

LORD MACAULAY'S LAYS of ANCIENT ROME. With 90 Illustrations on Wood, from the Antique, from Drawings by G. SCHARF. Fcp. 4to. 21s.

Miniature Edition of Lord Macaulay's Lays of Ancient Rome, with the Illustrations (as above) reduced in Lithography. Imp. 16mo. 10s. 6d.

The ÆNEID of VIRGIL Translated into English Verse. By JOHN CONINGTON, M.A. New Edition. Crown 8vo. 9s.

HORATII OPERA. Library Edition, with Marginal References and English Notes. Edited by the Rev. J. E. YONGE. 8vo. 21s.

The LYCIDAS and EPITAPHIUM DAMONIS of MILTON. Edited, with Notes and Introduction (including a Reprint of the rare Latin Version of the Lycidas, by W. Hogg, 1694), by C. S. JERRAM, M.A. Crown 8vo. 2s. 6d.

BOWDLER'S FAMILY SHAKSPEARE, cheaper Genuine Editions. Medium 8vo. large type, with 36 WOODCUTS, price 14s. Cabinet Edition, with the same ILLUSTRATIONS, 6 vols. fcp. 8vo. price 21s.

POEMS. By JEAN INGELOW. 2 vols. fcp. 8vo. price 10s. FIRST SERIES, containing 'DIVIDED,' 'The STAR'S MONUMENT,' &c. Sixteenth Thousand. Fcp. 8vo. price 5s. SECOND SERIES, 'A STORY of DOOM,' 'GLADYS and her ISLAND,' &c. Fifth Thousand. Fcp. 8vo. price 5s.

POEMS by Jean Ingelow. FIRST SERIES, with nearly 100 Illustrations, engraved on Wood by Dalziel Brothers. Fcp. 4to. 21s.

Rural Sports, &c.

DOWN the ROAD; Or, Reminiscences of a Gentleman Coachman. By C. T. S. BIRCH REYNARDSON. Second Edition, with Twelve Coloured Illustrations from Paintings by H. Alken. Medium 8vo. 21s.

The DEAD SHOT; or, Sportsman's Complete Guide: a Treatise on the Use of the Gun, Dog-breaking, Pigeon-shooting, &c. By MARKSMAN. Revised Edition. Fcp. 8vo. with Plates, 5s.

ENCYCLOPÆDIA of RURAL SPORTS; a complete Account, Historical, Practical, and Descriptive, of Hunting, Shooting, Fishing, Racing, and all other Rural and Athletic Sports and Pastimes. By D. P. BLAINE. With above 600 Woodcuts (20 from Designs by JOHN LEECH). 8vo. 21s.

The FLY-FISHER'S ENTOMOLOGY. By ALFRED RONALDS. With coloured Representations of the Natural and Artificial Insect. Sixth Edition, with 20 coloured Plates. 8vo. 14s.

A BOOK on ANGLING; a complete Treatise on the Art of Angling in every branch. By FRANCIS FRANCIS. New Edition, with Portrait and 15 other Plates, plain and coloured. Post 8vo. 15s.

WILCOCKS'S SEA-FISHERMAN; comprising the Chief Methods of Hook and Line Fishing, a Glance at Nets, and Remarks on Boats and Boating. New Edition, with 80 Woodcuts. Post 8vo. 12s. 6d.

HORSES and STABLES. By Colonel F. FITZWYGRAM, XV. the King's Hussars. With Twenty-four Plates of Illustrations, containing very numerous Figures engraved on Wood. 8vo. 10s. 6d.

The HORSE'S FOOT, and HOW to KEEP it SOUND. By W. MILES, Esq. Ninth Edition, with Illustrations. Imperial 8vo. 12s. 6d.

A PLAIN TREATISE on HORSE-SHOEING. By W. MILES, Esq. Sixth Edition. Post 8vo. with Illustrations, 2s. 6d.

STABLES and STABLE-FITTINGS. By W. MILES, Esq. Imp. 8vo. with 13 Plates, 15s.

REMARKS on HORSES' TEETH, addressed to Purchasers. By W. MILES, Esq. Post 8vo. 1s. 6d.

The HORSE: with a Treatise on Draught. By WILLIAM YOUATT. New Edition, revised and enlarged. 8vo. with numerous Woodcuts, 12s. 6d.

The DOG. By WILLIAM YOUATT. 8vo. with numerous Woodcuts, 6s.

The DOG in HEALTH and DISEASE. By STONEHENGE. With 70 Wood Engravings. Square crown 8vo. 7s. 6d.

The GREYHOUND. By STONEHENGE. Revised Edition, with 25 Portraits of Greyhounds. Square crown 8vo. 15s.

The OX; his Diseases and their Treatment: with an Essay on Parturition in the Cow. By J. R. DOBSON. Crown 8vo. with Illustrations, 7s. 6d.

Works of *Utility* and *General Information.*

The THEORY and PRACTICE of BANKING. By H. D. MACLEOD, M.A. Barrister-at-Law. Third and Cheaper Edition, revised. (In Two Volumes.) VOL. I. 8vo. price 12s.

M'CULLOCH'S DICTIONARY, Practical, Theoretical, and Historical, of Commerce and Commercial Navigation. New and revised Edition. 8vo. 63s.

The CABINET LAWYER; a Popular Digest of the Laws of England, Civil, Criminal, and Constitutional: intended for Practical Use and General Information. Twenty-fifth Edition. Fcp. 8vo. price 9s.

PROTECTION from FIRE and THIEVES. Including the Construction of Locks, Safes, Strong-Room, and Fire-proof Buildings; Burglary and the Means of Preventing it; Fire, its Detection, Prevention, and Extinction; &c. By G. H. CHUBB, Assoc. Inst. C.E. With 32 Woodcuts. Crown 8vo. 5s.

BLACKSTONE ECONOMISED, a Compendium of the Laws of England to the Present time, in Four Books, each embracing the Legal Principles and Practical Information contained in their respective volumes of Blackstone, supplemented by Subsequent Statutory Enactments, Important Legal Decisions, &c. By D. M. AIRD, Barrister-at-Law. Revised Edition. Post 8vo. 7s. 6d.

PEWTNER'S COMPREHENSIVE SPECIFIER; a Guide to the Practical Specification of every kind of Building-Artificers' Work, with Forms of Conditions and Agreements. Edited by W. YOUNG. Crown 8vo. 6s.

COLLIERIES and COLLIERS; a Handbook of the Law and Leading Cases relating thereto. By J. C. FOWLER. Third Edition. Fcp. 8vo. 7s. 6d.

HINTS to MOTHERS on the MANAGEMENT of their HEALTH during the Period of Pregnancy and in the Lying-in Room. By the late THOMAS BULL, M.D. Fcp. 8vo. 5s.

The MATERNAL MANAGEMENT of CHILDREN in HEALTH and Disease. By the late THOMAS BULL, M.D. Fcp. 8vo. 5s.

The THEORY of the MODERN SCIENTIFIC GAME of WHIST. By WILLIAM POLE, F.R.S. Fifth Edition, enlarged. Fcp. 8vo. 2s. 6d.

CHESS OPENINGS. By F. W. LONGMAN, Balliol College, Oxford. Second Edition revised. Fcp. 8vo. 2s. 6d.

THREE HUNDRED ORIGINAL CHESS PROBLEMS and STUDIES. By JAMES PIERCE, M.A. and W. T. PIERCE. With numerous Diagrams. Square fcp. 8vo. 7s. 6d. SUPPLEMENT, price 2s. 6d.

A PRACTICAL TREATISE on BREWING; with Formulæ for Public Brewers, and Instructions for Private Families. By W. BLACK. 8vo. 10s. 6d.

MODERN COOKERY for PRIVATE FAMILIES, reduced to a System of Easy Practice in a Series of carefully-tested Receipts. By ELIZA ACTON. Newly revised and enlarged; with 8 Plates and 150 Woodcuts. Fcp. 8vo. 6s.

MAUNDER'S TREASURY of KNOWLEDGE and LIBRARY of Reference; comprising an English Dictionary and Grammar, Universal Gazetteer, Classical Dictionary, Chronology, Law Dictionary, a synopsis of the Peerage useful Tables, &c. Revised Edition. Fcp. 8vo. 6s. cloth, or 10s. calf.

Knowledge for the Young.

The STEPPING-STONE to KNOWLEDGE; or upwards of 700 Questions and Answers on Miscellaneous Subjects, adapted to the capacity of Infant minds. 18mo. 1s.

SECOND SERIES of the STEPPING-STONE to KNOWLEDGE: Containing upwards of 800 Questions and Answers on Miscellaneous Subjects not contained in the FIRST SERIES. 18mo. 1s.

The STEPPING-STONE to GEOGRAPHY: Containing several Hundred Questions and Answers on Geographical Subjects. 18mo. 1s.

The **STEPPING-STONE** to **ENGLISH HISTORY**; Questions and Answers on the History of England. 18mo. 1s.

The **STEPPING-STONE** to **BIBLE KNOWLEDGE**; Questions and Answers on the Old and New Testaments. 18mo. 1s.

The **STEPPING-STONE** to **BIOGRAPHY**; Questions and Answers on the Lives of Eminent Men and Women. 18mo. 1s.

The **STEPPING-STONE** to **IRISH HISTORY**: Containing several Hundred Questions and Answers on the History of Ireland. 18mo. 1s.

The **STEPPING-STONE** to **FRENCH HISTORY**: Containing several Hundred Questions and Answers on the History of France. 18mo. 1s.

The **STEPPING-STONE** to **ROMAN HISTORY**: Containing several Hundred Questions and Answers on the History of Rome. 18mo. 1s.

The **STEPPING-STONE** to **GRECIAN HISTORY**: Containing several Hundred Questions and Answers on the History of Greece. 18mo. 1s.

The **STEPPING-STONE** to **ENGLISH GRAMMAR**: Containing several Hundred Questions and Answers on English Grammar. 18mo. 1s.

The **STEPPING-STONE** to **FRENCH PRONUNCIATION** and **CON-**VERSATION : Containing several Hundred Questions and Answers. 18mo. 1s.

The **STEPPING-STONE** to **ASTRONOMY**: Containing several Hundred familiar Questions and Answers on the Earth and the Solar and Stellar Systems. 18mo. 1s.

The **STEPPING-STONE** to **MUSIC**: Containing several Hundred Questions on the Science ; also a short History of Music. 18mo. 1s.

The **STEPPING-STONE** to **NATURAL HISTORY**: VERTEBRATE OR BACK-BONED ANIMALS. PART I. *Mammalia*; PART II. *Birds, Reptiles, and Fishes*. 18mo. 1s. each Part.

THE **STEPPING-STONE** to **ARCHITECTURE**; Questions and Answers explaining the Principles and Progress of Architecture from the Earliest Times. With 100 Woodcuts. 18mo. 1s.

INDEX.

Spottiswoode & Co., Printers New-street Square, London.